Leonard Merrick

The Man Who Was Good

A novel. Part 2

Leonard Merrick

The Man Who Was Good
A novel. Part 2

ISBN/EAN: 9783337049379

Printed in Europe, USA, Canada, Australia, Japan

Cover: Foto ©Andreas Hilbeck / pixelio.de

More available books at **www.hansebooks.com**

THE MAN WHO WAS GOOD

VOL. II.

THE MAN WHO WAS GOOD

A Novel

BY

LEONARD MERRICK

AUTHOR OF 'VIOLET MOSES,' 'MR. BAZALGETTE'S AGENT,'
ETC.

IN TWO VOLUMES

VOL. II.

London

CHATTO & WINDUS, PICCADILLY
1892

'That is the doctrine, simple, ancient, true ;
Such is life's trial, as old earth smiles and knows.
If you loved only what were worth your love,
Love were clear gain, and wholly well for you.'
James Lee's Wife.

CHAPTER VIII.

SLOWLY there stole into Kincaid's life a new interest.
He began to be more eager to visit the Lodge, was
sometimes sensible of an odd reluctance to rise and
go—even found the picture of the little drawing-
room, with its ease and lamplight, lingering with
him after the front door had closed. He was conscious in the atmosphere of an added charm, a
grace whose lack he had scarcely noted, but which
discovered the deficiency it supplied. A colour had
been diffused over the baldness of the home-
comings, quickening their somewhat elementary
colloquies, the accustomed questions, the renewed

assurances, into the vitality of conversation. He
had accepted the baldness as a matter of course,
reflecting that, strong as his attachment was for
his mother—indubitable as was hers for him—the
level dulness of her solitude, and the dearth of
gossip with himself, put a range of topics beyond
reach. Latterly, however, his tongue had moved
more freely in the reunions; subjects occurred
to him without the labour of research, and the
gaps in the discourse, which had often been but
awkwardly bridged, were now avoided altogether
by a different route.

It was, perhaps, to go beneath the surface of
things, a shade pathetic that the relations of
mother and son should have been stimulated by
the introduction of a stranger; but if Mrs. Kincaid
indeed connected Miss Brettan with the novel
briskness of the parlance, it was only by attributing to her companionship an improvement in
her own spirits which rendered her more conver-
sationally disposed. The sources of reforms, more-

over, are seldom investigated, people being addicted to receiving them in unanalytical content, and reserving their inquiries for retrogressions.

Nevertheless, if the understanding between the pair had been wholly complete, no stranger would have been capable of effecting the change which both remarked, and the man especially welcomed. The sameness of the subject-matter would have been diversified by the manner of its presentment. The fact was that, with all her affection for her son, the heart of Mrs. Kincaid remained outside her allusions to the profession which engrossed him. She was proud to have a doctor for a son, but vaguely : the career made no particular appeal to her, and an acquaintance with its details had seemed to her mind to really preclude the possibility of any great enthusiasm. Despite her goodness, she was, so far as he was concerned, wanting in that which can only be described as sympathy, though the word covers too much. It was just that subtlety of sympathy which affection *per se* is inadequate to create, and for whose birth love must co-operate with comprehension.

Personally Kincaid credited the full measure of the cheerier order of affairs to Miss Brettan's account, and regarded her engagement as a capital day's work. But between esteeming her responsible for the cheerfulness he found invigorating, and detecting it was she whose society invigorated him, lay a distance he did not immediately accomplish.

Summer had deepened into autumn, and winter was at hand, before he had plainly admitted to himself he liked to go to see Miss Brettan, and felt a sentiment of friendship for her. He had not readily separated the person from the surroundings in which he saw her. The cosiness of the room, with two women smiling at him when he entered —always with a little surprise, for the time of his coming was uncertain—and getting tea for him, and being sorry when he had to leave them, had pleased his fancy, and it had been a process to remember her as an individual instead of as an element of the scene. It was by degrees he realized how many of his expressions of opinion were in reality directed to her, how many of the opinions would never have been expressed without her, and, grown cognizant of it, a flavour was imparted to his existence which had been wanting. His one friendship had been for Corri, and Corri was not here. It is scarcely too much to pronounce the months following, when his cordial liking for Miss Brettan was clear to him, and possessed of a fascination due very largely to its unexpectedness, the happiest Kincaid had known.

The development was less serene, but it was fortunately slow. Friendship does not trouble itself with questions; it debates neither its wisdom nor its return. It is only the warmer stage of interest that wants to know so much, and insists on the *quid pro quo* in feeling. When he advanced to the higher temperature Kincaid first tasted uneasiness.

It commenced oddly. He had gone to the house earlier than was his habit, and the women were

preparing for a walk. Mary stood by the mantelpiece. There was something they had meant to
do; she said she would go alone to do it. He lay
back in the depths of an armchair, and watched
her while she spoke to his mother, watched the
play of her features and the quick turn of her
cheek. Then—it was the least significant of trivi-
alities—she plucked a hairpin from her hair, and
began to button her glove. It was revealed to him
as he contemplated her that she was eminently
lovable. His eyes dwelt on the tender curve of her
figure, displayed by the flexion of her arm; he
remarked the bend of the head, and the delicate
modelling of her ear and neck. These things were
quite new to him. He was stirred abruptly with
the magic of her sex. The admiration did not
last ten seconds, and before he saw her again he
only recollected it once, quite suddenly. But the
development had begun.

In his next visit he looked to see these beauties,
and found them. This time, being voluntary, the

admiration lasted longer. It was recurrent all the evening. He discovered a novel excellence in her performance of the simplest acts, and an additional enjoyment in talking with her. Perhaps it was, after all, wrong to declare his development a descent in satisfaction ; in its initial period he was very happy. The child's bow is such a toy that the prick of his arrow only tickles us pleasantly, and the puncture is old before we suffer from the poison at the point. Yes, Kincaid was surprisingly happy in the birth of his love for Miss Brettan ; it did him good.

Thoughts of her came to him while he sat at night-time in his room. The bare little apartment witnessed all the phases of the man's love —its brightness, and then its misgivings. He had no confidant to prose to—he could never have spoken of this strange new thing which had happened to him under any circumstances. He used to sit and think of her alone, wondering if God would put it into her heart to care for him, wondering in all humility if it could be ordained that he should ever hold this dear woman in his arms and call her ' wife.'

He would not be in a position to give her luxury, and for a couple of years he certainly could not marry at all ; but he believed primarily that he could at least give her content, and in reflecting what she would make of life for him he smiled. The salary he drew from his post was not a very large one, but his mother's means sufficed for her requirements, and he was able to lay almost the whole of it aside. He thought, when a couple of years had gone by, he would be justified in furnishing a small house, and that he might reasonably expect, through the introductions his appointment had procured him, to establish a practice. It would be rather pinched for them at first, of course, but she would not mind that much if she were fond of him. 'Fond' of him ! She 'fond' of him ! Could it be possible? he asked himself—Miss Brettan fond of him ! She was so composed, so quiet, she seemed such a long way off now that he wanted her for his own. Would it really ever happen that the woman whose hand had merely touched him in courtesy would one day be uttering words of love for him, and saying 'my husband'?

He wrestled long with his tenderness; the misgivings came quickly. After all, she was comfortable as she was—she was provided for, she had no pecuniary cares here. Had he the right to beg her to relinquish this comparative ease, and struggle by his side oppressed by the worries of a precarious income? Then, he told himself, they might take in patients: that would augment the income. And she was a dependant now; if she married him she would be her own mistress. He weighed all the pros and cons; he was no boy to call the recklessness of self-indulgence the splendour of devotion. He balanced the arguments on either side long and carefully. If he asked her to come to him, it should be with the conviction he was doing her no wrong. He saw how easy it would be to deceive himself, and to feel persuaded that the fact of her being in a situation made matrimony an advance to her, whether she wedded well or ill. He debated the advisability of owning his love as judicially as though he were sure of receiving hers if he did. He would act on no impulse, and perhaps spoil her life through impatience to learn how he stood with her before he had determined whether the confession would be fair. But he was very impatient. Through months he used to come away after every visit to the Lodge striving to discern importance in some answer or another she had made him, some question she had put to him, some gesture that could have meant a great deal or just nothing at all. It appeared to him that he had loved her much longer than he had; and he had made no progress. There were moments when he upbraided himself for being clumsy and stupid; some men in his place, he thought, would have divined what her feelings were long ago. And if, indeed, she had an affection for him, that

would settle the problem he could not succeed in
solving unaided. If she felt for him a tithe of
what he felt for her, it would be gentler to ask her
to share his responsibilities than to let her remain
unwooed. But did she? could she? Over and
over the beaten ground he went: Could she? did
she?

He never queried the wisdom of marrying her on
his own account: the privilege of cherishing her in
health and nursing her in sickness, of having her
head pillowed on his breast, and confiding his
hopes to her sympathy; of going through life with
her in a union in which she would give to him all
her inward self—the sacred and withheld identity
which no one but a husband can ever explore in a
woman—looked to him a joy for which he could
never be less than intensely and unspeakably grateful as long as the life endured. He ceased to
marvel at the birth of his love, it looked natural
now; she seemed to belong to Westport so wholly
by this time. He no longer contrasted the present

atmosphere of the villa with the duller atmosphere she had banished. He had forgotten that duller atmosphere. She was there—it was as if she had always been there. To reflect that there had been a period when he had known no Mary Brettan was strange. He wondered he had not felt the want of her. The day he met her in Corri's office appeared to him dim in the mists of at least five years. The exterior of the man, and the yearnings within him—Kincaid as he knew himself, and the doctor as he was known to the hospital—were so at variance that the incongruity would have been ludicrous if it had not been beautiful.

When Mary saw he had begun to care for her, it was the greatest tremor of insecurity she had experienced since the date of her arrival. She had foretasted many disasters in the interval, been harassed by many fears, but that Dr. Kincaid might fall in love with her was a contingency that had never entered her head. It was so utterly unexpected that for a week she had discredited the

evidence of her senses, and when the truth was
too palpable to be blinked any longer, her remaining hope was that he might decide never to speak.
Here the meditations of the man and the woman
were concerned with the same theme—both revolved the claims of silence, but from different
standpoints. His consideration was whether
avowal was unjust to her; she sustained herself by
attributing to him a reluctance to commit himself
to a woman of whom he knew so little. She clung
to this haven she had found; her refusal, if
indeed he did propose to her, would surely
necessitate her relinquishing it. Mrs. Kincaid
might not desire to see her 'companion' marry
her son, but still less would she desire to retain a
companion who had rejected him. It had been
as peaceful here as any place could be for her now,
felt Mary; the thought of being driven forth to do
battle with the world again terrified her. She
wondered if Mrs. Kincaid had 'noticed anything';
it was hard to believe she could have avoided it,

but she had evinced no sign of suspicion : her manner was the same as usual.

With the complication which had arisen to disturb her, the woman perceived how prematurely old she was. Her courage had all gone, she told herself; she said she had passed the capability for any sustained effort; and it was a fact that the uneventful tenor of the life she had been leading, congenial because it demanded no energy, had done much to render her lassitude permanent. Her pain, the rawness of it, had dulled—she could touch the wound now without writhing; but it had left her wearied unto death. To attempt to forget had been beyond her; recollection continued to be her secret luxury, and the inertia permitted by her position lent itself so thoroughly to a dual exist- ence, that to her own mind she had often seemed to be living more acutely in her reminiscences than in her intercourse with the lady whom she served.

From the commencement of the tour, which had

started in the autumn of the preceding year, she
had kept herself posted in Carew's movements as
regularly as was practicable. It was frequently
very difficult for her to gain access to a theatrical
paper; but generally she contrived to see one somehow, if not on the day it reached the town, then
later, and read the meagre chronicle of his doings
with avidity. She knew what parts he played,
and what cities he was visiting. It was a morbid
fascination, but to see his name mentioned nearly
every week, and to be able to know where he
was, appeared to her a ray of sunshine for which
she owed her one debt of thankfulness to his
profession. If he had been anything but an
actor, if the man could have gone abroad or
died, without it being possible for her to be aware
of it, she thought her situation would have been
too hideous for words. To steal that weekly
glimpse of the paper was her weekly glimmer
of sensation; sometimes the past seemed actually
to leap into life again as the familiar capitals met

her gaze, and she was momentarily in the old surroundings once more.

There had only been two tours, and after the
second she had watched his ' card ' anxiously to
ascertain the proposed arrangements for the next.
Three months had slipped away while she watched
it, and between his and his agent's name nothing
had been added but the ' Resting.'

At last, one day after she had been reading from
the London newspaper to Mrs. Kincaid, and was
sitting silent with it lying on her lap, she had
derived some further information. A word of the
theatrical gossip had caught her eye, and, unperceived by the old lady, she started violently. She
had seen ' Seaton Carew.' For a minute she could
not quell her agitation sufficiently to pick the paper
up and peruse the paragraph ; she sat staring down
at it and deciphering nothing. When she raised it
at length, she learnt that Miss Olive Westland and
her husband, Mr. Seaton Carew, encouraged by
their successes in the provinces, had decided to

make a bid for the favour of Metropolitan audiences, and had completed negotiations by which the Boudoir Theatre would be opened under their management at the end of the ensuing month. It was added that this of late unfortunate house was to be redecorated, and a reference to an artist or two already engaged showed Mary that Carew was playing with big stakes.

Thenceforward she had had a new medium of intelligence, and one attainable without trouble, for the London paper was delivered at the Lodge daily. As the date for the production drew near, her impatience to hear the verdict on its merits had grown so strong that the superficial calm of her demeanour often threatened to break down. The walls of the country parlour cooped her; she saw through them into the city beyond, saw on to a draughty stage dimly lighted at a rehearsal which Carew was conducting.

The piece had failed; on the morning when she

learned it had failed she had dumbly participated in the chagrin of the failure. ' Yes ' and ' No ' she had answered, and seen with the eyes of her heart the gloom of a man's face she had once been used to press against her own. She did not care, she vowed ; her sole feeling with regard to the undertaking had been curiosity — if it had been more than curiosity she would despise herself; but her countenance was shadowed notwithstanding, and very perfunctory indeed was the tone of her replies.

She continued to scan the Boudoir advertisement every day, and it was not long before she had ascertained that another venture was in preparation. And she held more skeins of wool, and watched with veiled eagerness this advertisement develop like its predecessor. Recently the play had been produced, and the ' notice ' had been read by her in Mrs. Kincaid's presence. When she finished it she knew that Carew's hopes were over—that unless the capital of which his marriage had possessed him was far larger than had been believed, the season at the Boudoir would see it exhausted. There were no high encomiums passed upon his performance, either : he was dismissed in an indifferent sentence like his wife. Praise for his acting, which might have procured him Metropolitan engagements, had not been accorded, and as artist as well as manager his attempt had fallen to the ground.

When Kincaid, who little dreamed of the past which was flooding the woman's brain, went round to the house one evening, the servant told him his mother had already gone to her room, and that Miss Brettan was sitting with her. She was not feeling well, the girl added in explanation.

' Say I'm here, please,' he requested, ' and ask if I may come up.'

As he spoke Miss Brettan came down the stairs.

' Ah, doctor,' she said ; ' Mrs. Kincaid has gone to bed.'

' So I hear. What's the matter with her ?'

'Only neuralgia; she has had it all day. She has just fallen asleep.'

'Then I had better not go up to see her?'

'I don't think I would, if I were you; it would be a pity to disturb her. I have just come down to get a book.'

'You are going to sit in her room?'

'Yes ; in case she wakens of her own accord.'

They stood speaking in the hall, outside the parlour door.

'Where is your book?' he said.

'Inside. I am sorry you should have come round for nothing; Mrs. Kincaid will be so disappointed when she hears about it. May I tell her you will come again to-morrow?'

'Yes, I'll look round some time during the day, if it's only for a moment. I think I'll sit down awhile before I go.'

'Will you?' she said. 'I beg your pardon.'

She opened the door, and he followed her into the room.

'You won't mind my leaving you?' she inquired. 'I don't want to remain away from your mother, lest she *should* want anything.'

It was nearly dark in the parlour; the lamp had not been lighted, and the fire was low. A little snow whitened the laburnum-tree which was visible through the window. It was an evening in January, and Mary had been in Westport now nearly two years.

'Can you see to find the book?' he said. 'Where did you leave it?'

'It was on the sideboard; Ellen must have moved it, I expect. I'll ask her where she's put it.'

'No, don't do that; I'll light the lamp for you.'

She lifted the globe while he struck a match. It was his last, and it went out.

'Never mind,' he said; 'we'll get a light from the fire.'

'Oh,' she exclaimed, 'but I'm giving you so much trouble; you had better let me call the girl!'

A dread of what might happen in this darkness

was coming over her. 'You had much better let me call the girl,' she repeated.

'Try if you can get a light with this first,' he said; 'see, I'll shift that lump of ash; press it in where the coals are red.'

She stooped over the grate, one hand holding the twist of paper, the other resting on the mantelpiece. He leant beside her, shifting the embers with his foot.

It flashed back at her, as the foot went to and fro, how Tony had stood at a mantelpiece kicking the faded embers that night in Leicester, while he was breaking his news. A sickening anxiety swept through her to get away from Kincaid before he could have a chance to touch her. The paper charred and curled in the heat without catching a flame, and in her impatience she hated him for the delay. She detested herself for being here, lingering in the gloaming with a man who had dared to feel about her in the same way that once upon a time Tony had felt.

She rose abruptly.

'It's no use, doctor; Ellen will have to do the work, after all.'

'Don't go just yet,' he said; 'I want to speak to you, Miss Brettan.'

'I cannot stay any longer,' she declared. 'I——'

'You will give me a minute? There is something I have been waiting to say to you; I have been waiting a long while.'

She raised her face to him. In the shadows which filled the room he could see little more of it than her eyes.

'Don't say it,' she replied. 'I think that I can guess, perhaps . . . Don't say it, Dr. Kincaid!'

'Yes!' he insisted, 'I must do that—I must say it, and you shall give me your answer then; I am bound to tell you before I take your answer, Mary. My dear, I love you!'

'Oh, you wanton!' she shivered; 'you degraded, horrible thing!'

'If you can't care for me, you have only to tell

me so to-night; it shall never be a worry to you.
I would not have my love become a worry to you,
to make you wish I were not here. But if you can
care, in time, a little . . . if you think that when
I am able to ask you to come to me you could
come . . . oh, my dear one, all my life I will be
tender to you—all my life !'

He could not see her eyes any longer ; her head
was bent upon her bosom, and in her silence the
tall man trembled.

The servant came in with the taper, kindling the
lamp and letting down the blinds. They stood on
the hearth watching her dumbly while she moved
about. And when the blinds were lowered she
screwed the wicks higher, so that the room was
bright; and then Kincaid turned his gaze towards
the woman's face, and yearned over its pale-
ness.

'Is there anything else, miss ?'

'No, Ellen, thank you; I think that's all.'

'Mary!' he said.

'I am so sorry. You cannot think how sorry I am to have brought you pain.'

'You could never care—not ever so little—for me?'

'Not in that way: no.'

He looked away from her—looked at the engraving of Wellington and Blucher meeting on the field of Waterloo; stared at the filter on the sideboard, through which the water fell drop by drop. A heavy weight seemed to have come suddenly down upon him, so that he breathed under it laboriously. He wanted to speak in order to curtail the pause, which he understood must be trying to her; but he could not think of anything to say, nor could he shake his brain clear of her last words, which appeared to him incessantly reiterated. He felt as if his hope of her had been something vital, and she had stamped it out, to leave him confronting a new beginning, so strange that time must elapse before it would be possible for him to realize how wholly strange it was going to be. Even while he strove to address her it was difficult to feel that she was still very close to him. Her tones lingered; the dress she wore emphasized itself upon his consciousness more and more; but from her presence he had a curious sensation of being remote. Like the perspective of a landscape, she seemed no less distant because he knew that she was near.

'Good-night,' he said at length abruptly. 'You mustn't let this thing trouble you, you know. I shall always be glad I am fond of you; I shall always be glad I told you so: I was hoping until I spoke, and now I understand. It's so much better to understand than to go on hoping for what never can come.'

She searched pityingly for something kind; but the futility of phrases daunted her.

'I had better close the door after you,' she murmured, 'or it will make a noise.'

They went out into the passage, and stood together on the step.

'It's beginning to snow again,' he remarked; 'it

looks as if we were going to have a heavy fall.'

' Yes,' she said dully, glancing at the sky.

She put out her hand, and it lay for an instant in his.

' Once more, Miss Brettan, good-night.'

' Good-night to you, Dr. Kincaid.'

As he reached the path he turned, in bowing to her; she was silhouetted against the gaslight of the hall. Then her figure was withdrawn, and the view of the interior was narrowed, until, while he looked back, the brightness vanished altogether and the door was shut.

CHAPTER IX.

AND so it was all over.

'All over,' he said to himself—'over and done with, Philip! Steady yourself, Philip; put a front on it, and take it fighting!'

But they were only words—as yet he could not 'take it fighting'—they meant nothing. It was too soon; his hope had been slaughtered too newly. Nor was the knowledge that he was never going to hold her—the feeling that the air-castles habitation had made homely had melted into mist—quite all the grief which lay upon him as he made his way along the ill-lit streets. There was, besides, a very cruel smart—the abstract pain of being such a little to one who was so much to him.

He paid his visit to the wards that night with it hidden where it burned. Those of the patients who were still awake had the doctor at their bedsides; and he dressed such wounds as needed to be dressed, and heard the little peevish questions and the dull complaints just as he had done the night before. The nurse walked softly past the sleepers with her shaded lamp, the travelling light along the length of darkness, and once or twice he spoke a word to her—this also like the night before. And when, the doctor's duties done, the man had gained the room where the memories of Mary always dwelt with him, he thought of that night before, and sat with elbows on the table while the hours struck, remembering what had happened since.

The necessity for returning to the house so speedily, to see his mother, was eminently distasteful; he longed to escape it. And then he suddenly warmed towards her in self-reproach, thinking it had been very hard of him to wish to neglect his

mother in order to spare awkwardness to another
woman. His repugnance to the task was deep-
rooted, all the same, nor did it lessen as the afternoon approached. But for the fact of yesterday's
indisposition, he could never have brought himself
to overcome it.

The embarrassment he had feared, however, was
avoided by Miss Brettan's absence. When he
entered she was out of the room, and, struggling
with a growing anxiety to ask after her, he sat
awhile in the parlour, alternately hoping and
dreading she would come in. Mrs. Kincaid was
quite well again to-day, she declared; Mary had
told her of his call the previous evening; how long
was it he had stopped?

'Oh, not very long,' he said; 'has the neuralgia
quite gone?'

'I feel a little weary after it, that's all. Is there
anything fresh, Philip?'

'Fresh?' he answered vaguely; 'no, dear, I don't
know that there's anything very fresh.'

'You look tired yourself,' she said: 'I thought that perhaps you were troubled.'

She thought, too, Miss Brettan had looked troubled, and instinct pointed to something having occurred during the call which was not mentioned. A conviction that her son was getting fond of her companion had been unspoken in her mind for some time, and under her placid questions now rankled a little wistfulness in feeling that she was not held dear enough for confidence. She wanted to say to him outright: 'Philip, did you tell that woman you were fond of her when I was upstairs last night?' but was frightened to seem inquisitive, since he appeared to design her to remain outside the matter. He, with never an inkling she could suspect his love, meanwhile reflected how essential for Mary's continued peace it was that she should never conjecture he had been refused.

It is doubtful whether he had ever felt so wholly tender towards his mother as he did in these moments while he admitted that it was imperative for Mary's sake to keep the secret from her; and doubtful whether the mother's heart had ever turned so far aside from him as while she perceived that she was never to be told.

They exchanged commonplaces with the one grave subject throbbing in the mind of each. Of the two, perhaps the mother was the more laboured, so that presently he noticed what uphill work it was, and checked a sigh, to lapse into reverie from which he roused himself with an effort by fits and starts. She heard the sigh, and could have echoed it, meditating sadly that the presence of her companion was required now to make her society endurable to him. But she would not refer to Mary; she bent over her wool-work, and the needle went in and out with feeble regularity while she maintained a wounded silence which the man was regarding as an unwillingness to talk.

He said, at length, he must be going, and she did not offer to detain him.

' I want to hurry back this afternoon; you won't
mind ?'

' No,' she murmured; ' you know what you have
to do, Philip, better than I.'

He stooped and kissed her. For the first time
in her life she did not return his kiss. She gave
him her cheek, and rested one hand a little tremu-
lously on his shoulder.

' Good-bye,' she said ; her tone was so gentle he
did not remark the absence of the caress. ' Don't
go working too hard, Phil !'

He patted the hand reassuringly, and let himself
out. Then the hand crept slowly up to her eyes,
and she wiped some tears away. The wool-work
dropped to her lap, and she sat recalling a little
boy who had been used to talk of the wondrous
things he was going to do for ' mother ' when he
became a man, and who now had become a man,
living for a strange woman, and full of a love which
' mother ' might only guess.

She could not feel quite so cordial to Mary as

she had done. To think of her holding her son's
confidence, while she was left to speculate, made
the need for surmises seem harder. And Philip
was unhappy: her companion must be indifferent
to him; nothing but that could account for the unhappiness or for the reservation. She could have
forgiven her engrossing his affections—with time—
but her indifference was more than she could bring
herself to condone. Still, this was the woman he
loved, and in their daily intercourse she endeavoured to hide from her the chagrin she felt, as
she had hidden her suspicions. Perhaps it was,
though, that resentment was less easy to mask than
suspicion, or perhaps, during her retreat while his
visit was being paid, Mary's nervousness had inclined her to over-estimate the probabilities of dis-
closure, and so rendered her now very scrutinous
for signs of cognizance, for in the ensuing week
the communion between the pair had its hitches,
despite Mrs. Kincaid's determination. Their
parlance was scarcely so unrestricted as usual;

there were long pauses which seemed to Miss Brettan, dwelling on its likelihood, emphatically significant of condemnation—often, indeed, to be preparatory to an onslaught of inquiry. She was exceedingly uncomfortable during this week, and was sometimes only deterred from yielding to an impulse to proclaim the fact of her rejection, and appeal to the other's fairness to exonerate her, by the recollection that it was, after all, just possible the avowal might have the effect of transforming a bush into an officer.

She could not venture to repeat the retirement to her room on the next occasion of the doctor's coming. Nearly a fortnight had gone by before he came ; and she forced herself to turn to him with a few remarks, made the more difficult by her apprehension of the mother's divination of their difficulty and the evident effort of respondency in him. He was not the man to be able to cover his feelings by a flow of small-talk, his life had not qualified him for it ; he could simply conceal

16—2

emotion, he could not feign jocundity, and it was
an ordeal to him sitting there in the presence of
Mary and witnessing attempts in which he painfully perceived himself so wholly unadapted to
co-operate. The knowledge that the simulated
ease should have originated with himself rather
than with her caused his want of concurrence to
seem additionally ungracious, and he feared she
must think him boorish, and disposed to parade his
disappointment for the purpose of exciting her
compassion.

Strongly, therefore, as he had desired to avoid a
break in the social routine, his subsequent visits
were made at longer intervals, and more often than
not curtailed on the plea of work. It was as yet,
at all events, clearly impossible for him to behave
to her as if nothing untoward had happened, and,
wishful to convey the impression of restored
tranquillity, to shun the house awhile looked to him
at least a wiser course than to haunt it with dis-
composure patent. Thus the restraint which Mrs.

Kincaid was imposing upon herself had to bear a further burden ; Miss Brettan was driving her son from her side. The pauses became more frequent, and, to Mary, more than ever ominous. Indeed, while the mother mused mournfully on the consequences of her engagement, the companion herself was questioning how long she could expect to retain it. She began to consider whether she ought not to relinquish it of her own accord, to elude the indignity of a dismissal. Even if Mrs. Kincaid did fail to suspect the reason of her son absenting himself in this fashion, her responsibility was just the same, she reflected. It was she who divided the pair, and who was accountable for the hurt expression her employer's countenance now so constantly assumed. She felt wearily that women had a great deal to endure in life, what with the men they cared for, and the men for whom they did not care. There seemed no privileges pertaining to their sex ; being feminine only amplified the scope for vexation. A fact she did not see was

that one of the most pathetic things in connection
with the unloved lover is the irritability with which
the woman so often thinks about him.

With what sentiments she might have listened
to Kincaid's suit had she met him prior to her
intimacy with Carew there is no means of con-
jecturing. Now he touched her not at all; but the
intimacy had been an experience which engulfed
so much of her sensibility, that to speculate upon
her attitude as it might have been had her passion
and her fall never occurred is akin to speculating
on the potentialities of a different being. Kincaid's
rival, in truth, was the most powerful one a lover
can ever oppose : the rival of a vivid remembrance
—always a doughty antagonist, and never so
impregnable as when the woman is instinctively a
good woman and has waived her goodness for the
sake of the man she is remembering.

The idea entered Mary's head of endeavouring to
secure an opportunity of speaking alone with the
doctor, and letting him know he was paining his

mother by so rarely coming now ; but such an opportunity was not easy to gain, for when he did come his mother of course was present. She thought of writing, but by word of mouth a suggestion would suffice, whilst a letter, considering her acquaintance with the cause, would have its awkwardness.

More than two months had gone by since the night of his proposal when Mrs. Kincaid made her plaint. It was on a Sunday morning. Mary was standing before the window looking out into the brightness of sunshine, while the elder woman sat moodily in her accustomed seat.

' Are we going to church ?' asked Mary presently.

' Yes, I suppose so ; there's plenty of time, is there not ?'

' Oh, it's early yet !—not ten. What a lovely day, isn't it ? The spring has begun in earnest.'

' Yes,' assented the other absently.

There was a short silence after the monosyllable, and then :

'I shall not run any risk of missing Dr. Kincaid by going out; he isn't such a frequent visitor that I need be afraid of that!'

Her addendum had in it so much more of pathos than of testiness, that after the instant of dismay her companion felt acutely sorry for her.

'A doctor's time is scarcely his own, is it?' she murmured, turning; 'there are so many calls upon it.'

Mrs. Kincaid did not reply immediately, and to Mary the delay seemed to accentuate the feebleness of her rejoinder.

'I mean,' she said, stumbling on in an effort to invigorate it, 'that it is not as if he were able to leave the hospital whenever he has the inclination. There may be cases——'

'He used to be able to come often; why should he not be able now?'

'Yes——' faltered Miss Brettan.

'I have not asked him; I can be sure it is a good reason that keeps him from me, of course; but it is hard, when you are living in the same town as your son, not to have him with you for longer than an hour in a month. I don't see much more of him than that, lately, you are aware. Yesterday-week he was here last; he stayed twenty minutes. The time before he said he was in a hurry before he said, "How do you do?" He never put his hat down—you may have noticed it?'

'Yes, I noticed it,' Miss Brettan admitted.

'You know; oh, you do know!' she cried inwardly, with a sinking of the heart. 'Now, what am I to do? Don't imagine I am blaming him,' pursued Mrs. Kincaid, 'I am not blaming any-body; the reason may be very powerful indeed. Only it seems rather unfair that I should have to suffer for it, considering that I am even ignorant what it is.'

'Then why not speak to Dr. Kincaid? If he understood you felt his absence so keenly, you may be sure he would try to come oftener. Why don't you tell him that you miss him?'

' I shall never sue to my son for his visits,' said the old lady with a touch of dignity, 'nor do I desire to find out why he stops away. That is quite his own affair. At my age we begin to see that our children have rights we mustn't intrude into—secrets which must be told to us freely by them, or not told at all. We begin to see it, only we are old to learn. There, my dear, don't let us talk about the subject, it's not an agreeable one ; I think we had better go and dress.'

Mary looked at her a little helplessly ; there was a finality in her tone which precluded the possibility of any advance, and threatened to leave them one each side of a wall which, if partially demolished by the reference, had also been approached by it.

It was more than ever manifest to Miss Brettan that the task of remonstrating with the doctor devolved upon herself, and she decided she would write him a note that afternoon. Shortly after dinner Mrs. Kincaid, tempted by the fineness of the day, went out into the garden, and, left to her own devices in the parlour, Mary drew her chair to the escritoire with this intention. She would write a few lines, she thought, however clumsy, and despatch them at once. Still, they were not easy lines to produce, and, the resolution to be slap-dash notwithstanding, she nibbled her pen a good deal in the course of their composition ; the self-conscious-ness which invaded some of the sentences was too glaring. Finished at last, she slipped the note into her pocket, and, joining the widow, announced a wish to go for a walk.

' Oh, by all means ; why not ?'

' I thought perhaps you might be wanting me,' she returned, not without chafing under the tie of servitude.

' No,' said Mrs. Kincaid ; ' I shall get along very well ; I'm gardening.'

She was, indeed, more cheerful than Mary had seen her for some while, busying herself among the violets, and stooping over the crocuses to clear the soil away.

'Go along,' she added, nodding across her shoulder; 'a walk will do you good.'

Though the wish for one had only been expressed to avoid the mediation of a servant, the pretext having been put forward, Mary thought she might advantageously avail herself of it, and, the missive posted, she extended her excursion as far as the beach.

Sauntering along, however, it struck her that, despite Mrs. Kincaid's assertion, the chances were rather in favour of the doctor making his over-due call that afternoon, and she regretted the probability had not occurred to her earlier. His mother being in the garden, she might have been able to convey her intimation to him verbally, and so have dispensed with the laboured letter. Chagrined at the oversight, she bent her way homeward, and, in view of the Lodge, perceived him in the act of quitting it. They came face to face not fifty yards from the door. In remembrance her letter now appeared more stupid than ever, and she would have given much to have postponed transmitting it.

'I heard you were walking,' he remarked as they stood fronting each other on the pavement ; ' have you been far ?'

' Not very,' she said; ' I changed my mind. How did you find your mother, doctor ?'

' She had been pottering about on the wet ground, which was none too wise of her. Why do you ask ?'

' I—she has been missing you a little, I think ; she wants you there more often.'

' Oh,' he said, ' I am very sorry ! Are you sure ?'

' Yes, I am sure; it is more than a little she misses you. In point of fact, I have just written to you, Dr. Kincaid.'

' To me ? What—about this ?'

' Yes.'

' I did not know,' he said; ' I never supposed she would miss me like that. It was very kind of you.'

'I wished to speak to you about it before. I have seen for some time she was distressed.'

'Has she said anything?'

'She only mentioned it this morning, but I have noticed.'

'It was very kind of you,' he repeated; 'I am much obliged.'

Both suffered slightly from the consciousness of suppression; and after a few seconds she said boldly:

'Dr. Kincaid, if you are staying away with any idea of sparing embarrassment to me, I beg that you will put me outside the matter altogether.'

'Of course,' he rejoined, 'I did suppose you found my coming unwelcome; I was afraid it must be.'

'But do you suppose I could consent to keep you from your mother's house? You must see—the responsibility of it! What I should like to know is: are you staying away solely for my sake?'

'I did not wish to intrude my trouble on you.'

'No,' she said; 'that is not what I mean. I am glad I have met you; I want to speak to you plainly. I have thought perhaps it hurt you to come; that my being there reminded—that you didn't like it. If that is so——'

' I think you are exaggerating the importance of the thing!' he declared. 'It is very nice and womanly of you, but you are making yourself unhappy without any reason. I have had a good deal to occupy me of late—for the future I shall go more often.'

'I feel very guilty,' she answered. 'If I am right in imagining it would be pleasanter for you to absent yourself than to go there and see me, my course is clear. It is not my home, you know; I am in a situation, and it can be given up.'

' You mustn't talk like that !' he answered. ' I must have blundered very badly to give you such an idea. Don't let us stand here. Do you mind turning back a little way ? If my confession to you obliged you to leave Westport, I should reproach myself for it bitterly.'

They strolled slowly down the street, and during a minute each of the pair sought phrases.

'It is certain,' she said abruptly, 'that my being your mother's companion is quite wrong.   If I were not in the house you would go there the same as formerly.   I can't help feeling that.'

'But I will go there the same as formerly,' he averred; 'I have said so!'

'Yes,' she murmured.

'Doesn't that satisfy you?'

'You will go, but the fact remains that you would rather not; and the cause of your reluctance is my presence there.'

'It is you who are insisting on the reluctance,' he replied evasively; '*I* have not said I am reluctant.   I thought you would prefer me to avoid you for a while; personally——'

'Oh!' she said, 'do you think I have not seen? I know very well the position is a false one!'

'I told you I would never become a worry to you,' he said humbly; 'I have been trying to keep my word.'

'You have been everything that is considerate; the fault is my own. I ought to have resigned my place with your mother the day after you spoke to me.'

'I don't think that would have helped me much,' he responded. 'You must understand that a change in your life like that was the very last thing I desired my love to effect.'

At the word 'love' the woman flinched a little, and he himself had not been void of sensation in uttering it. The sound of it was loud to both of them, but to her it added to the sense of awkwardness, while to the man it seemed to bring them nearer.

'It was very dense of me,' he went on; 'but with all the consequences of speaking to you that I foresaw, I never took into account the one that has happened. I wondered if I was justified in asking you to give up a comfortable livelihood for the cares of such a home as I could offer; I considered half a dozen things; but that I might be making the house unbearable to you I overlooked. Now, with your interest at heart all the time, I have injured you. I can't tell you how sorry I am to learn it!'

'It is not unbearable,' she said; 'unbearable is much too strong. But I do see my duty, and I know the right thing is for me to go away; your mother would have you then as she ought to have you. While I stop it can never be really free for either of you. And of course she knows.'

'Do you think she does?' he exclaimed.

'Are women blind? Of course she knows! And what can she feel towards me? It is only the affection she has for you that prevents her discharging me.'

'Oh, don't!' he said. 'Discharging you!'

'What am I? I am only her servant. Don't

blink facts, Dr. Kincaid; I am your mother's "companion," a woman you had never seen two years ago. It would have been a good deal better for you if you had never seen me at all!'

'You can't say what would have been best for *me*,' he replied unsteadily; 'I would rather have known you as I do than that we hadn't met. For yourself, perhaps——'

'Hush!' she interrupted; 'we can neither of us forget what our meeting was! For myself, I owe my very life to meeting you; that is why the result of it is so abominable—such a shame! I haven't said much, but I remember every day what I owe you. I know I owe you the very clothes I wear!'

'For Heaven's sake!' he muttered.

'And my repayment is to make you unhappy—and her unhappy. It is noble!'

Her pace quickened, and to see her excited acted upon him very strongly. He longed to comfort her, and because this was impossible by reason of

17—2

the disparity of their sentiments, the sight of her emotion was more painful. He had never felt the hopelessness of his attachment so heavy on him as now that he saw her disturbed on account of it, and realized at the same time that it debarred him from offering her consolation. They walked along, gazing before them fixedly into the vista of the shut-up shops and Sunday quietude, until at last he said with an effort :

‘If you did go you would make me unhappier than ever.’

She did not reply to this, and after a glance at the troubled profile :

‘I am ready to do whatever you want,’ he added ; ‘whatever will make the position easiest to you. It seems that, with the best intentions towards each of you, I have only succeeded in giving annoyance to you both. But the wrong to my mother can be remedied, and if you let me drive you away from the house I shall have done some lasting harm. Why don’t you say that you will remain ?’

'Because I am not sure about it. I can't determine.'

'Your objection was the fancy that you were responsible for my so seldom seeing her; I have promised I will see her as often as I can.'

She bit her lips, without speaking.

'I can't do any more—can I?'

'No,' she confessed.

'Then, what is the matter?'

'The matter is that——'

'Yes,' he said; 'what is it?'

'You show me more plainly every minute that I ought to go.'

Something in the dumbness with which this announcement was received told her how unexpected it had been. And, indeed, to hear that his love, unperceived by himself, had been fighting against him was the hardest thing he had had to bear. Sensible that every remonstrance he suffered to escape his lips could only estrange them further, the helplessness of his condition wrung the man.

They were now crossing the churchyard, and she said something about the impracticability of her going any farther.

'Since our talk will have the effect of taking you to the Lodge more frequently, Dr. Kincaid, it hasn't been useless.'

'Wait a second!' he said. He paused by the porch, and looked at her. 'I—I can't leave you like this—Mary!'

'Oh!' she faltered, 'don't say anything — don't!'

'I must; what is the good?—I keep back everything, and you still know! You will always know! Nothing could have been more honestly meant than my assurance that I would never bring distress to you, and I have brought distress. Let us look the thing squarely in the eyes: you won't be my wife, but you needn't go away. What would you do? Whom do you know? Leaving my loss of you out of the question, think of the self-reproach!'

Inside the church an outburst of children's voices, muffled somewhat by the shut door, but still too near to be wholly beautiful, rose suddenly in hymn. She stood with averted face, staring over the rankness of the grass the wind was stirring lightly among the gravestones.

'Let us look at the thing squarely for once,' he said again. 'We are both remembering I love you; nothing can really be gained by ignoring the fact. If the circumstances were different, if you had somewhere to go, I should have less right to interfere; but friendless as you are, your leaving would mean a constant shame to me. All the time I should be thinking: "She was at peace in a home, and you drove her out from it!" To see the woman he loves wander away to be adrift among strangers; knowing she goes unprotected; to want, perhaps, for the barest necessities—good heavens! do you suppose there is any man who could bear the sight? I should feel as if I had turned you out of doors.'

A sudden tremor seized her, so that she shivered as if with chill.

'Sit down,' he said authoritatively. 'We must come to an understanding.'

But his protest was not continued immediately, and in the shelter of the porch both were thoughtful. She was the first to speak again, after all.

'You are persuading me to be a great coward,' she said unsteadily, 'and I am not a very brave woman at the best. If I do what is right for us both, I may give you pain in the present, but I shall spare you the unhappiness you will have if you go on meeting me every day.'

'You consider my welfare and her welfare, but not your own. And why—you would spare me nothing!'

'You will never be satisfied. Oh, yes, let us be honest to each other. You are right: your misgivings about me are true enough; but you are principally anxious for me to stop that you may still see me. And what will come of it? I can never marry you, never; and you will be wretched. If I gave you a chance to forget——'

'I shall never forget, whether you stop or whether you go.'

'You *must* forget!' she cried. 'You must forget me till it is as if you had never known me. I will not be burdened with the knowledge that I am spoiling your life. I will not!'

'Mary!' he said appealingly.

'Oh,' she exclaimed, 'it is cruel! I wish to God I had died before you loved me!'

'You don't know what you are saying; you make me feel—— Why,' he demanded under his breath—'why could it never be—in time, if you stay? I will never speak of it any more till you permit it, not a sign shall tell you I am waiting; but by-and-by, if I am patient, will it be always impossible? Dearest, it holds me so fast, this love of you! Don't be harsher than you need be; it is so earnest, so deep. I am not a man to love twice; I never knew I was able to love at all until you taught me. Don't refuse me the right to hope—in secret, by myself: it is all I have, all I will ask of you for years, if you like—the right to think that sometime, perhaps, the day may come when I can take you to me and call you wife; leave me that !'

' I can't,' she said thickly ; ' it would be a lie.'

' You could never care for me—not so much as to let me care for you ?'

A movement answered him, and his head was lowered. He sat, his chin supported by his palm, watching the restless working of her hands upon her lap. The closing words of the hymn came out distinctly to them both, and they listened till the hush fell, without knowing that they listened.

' One question : I may be wrong to ask you, but your confidence, you know, will be—I shall respect. Will you tell me : is it because you love some other man ?'

' No, no,' she said vehemently, ' I do not love !'

' Thank God for that ! while your love is in your

own keeping my prayer will always be to win it.
So long as you are free you will remain the woman
I want and wait for to the end.'

Her hands lay quite still. The compulsion for
avowal was confronting her at last. To be told
this thing and to sanction it by leaving him
unenlightened was a guilt she dared not con-
template; and under the obligation to proclaim
that, though a tenderness were ever borne to her,
they would be divided still, she turned cold and
damp. Twice she attempted the finality required,
and twice her lips parted without sound.

'Dr. Kincaid!'

He lifted his eyes to her, and the courage faded.

'Don't think,' he said, 'that I shall ever make
you regret replying. You have taken a great
dread away from me, and that is all. I am grateful
to you.'

'Oh,' she murmured, in a suffocating voice,
'because I do not love is—how am I to explain the
—why don't you understand?'

' What is it I should understand ?'

' You cannot be grateful; you are mistaken—never in the world, so long as we live—there was someone else I——'

' Be fair with me,' he said sternly ; ' in common justice, let us have clearness and truth : you have just declared you did not care for anyone ?'

' No,' she gasped, ' I did say that—I meant, I did not care—I do not—we neither care; he does not know if I am alive, but—there used to be another man, and——'

' Oh, my God, you are going to tell me you are married !'

She shook her head. His eyes were piercing her ; she felt them on her wherever she looked.

' Then speak and be done ! " There was another man ;" what more ?'

Suddenly the first fear had entered his veins, and, though he was only conscious of a vague oppression, he was already terrified by the anticipation of what he was going to hear.

' " There was another man," ' he repeated
hoarsely. ' What of him ?'

She was leaning forward, stooping so that her
face was completely hidden. With the silence that
had fallen inside the church the scene seemed
quieter than it had been, and the stillness in the
air intensified her difficulty of speech. She struggled
to evolve from her confusion the phrase to express
her impurity: but all the terms looked shameless and
unutterable alike, and the travail continued until,
sick with the tension of the pause and the violent
beating of her heart, she said almost inaudibly :

' I lived with him three years.'

assurance appeared puerile to him, incongruous. There was an air almost of unreality about their being seated here as they were, gazing at the blur of churchyard. Something never to be undone had happened, and she was strange.

The service was ended, and, trooping through the door, the Sunday-school pupils clattered past their feet, shiny and clamorous, and eyeing them with sidelong inquisition. She rose nervously, and, rousing himself, he accompanied her between the crowd of children as far as the gate, where their paths diverged. There their steps flagged to a standstill, and for a few seconds both remained looking down the lane in silence.

To her, stunned by no shock to make reality less real, these final seconds held the condensed humiliation of the hour. The rigidity with which the man waited beside her seemed eloquent of disgust, and she mused bitterly on what she had done, how she had abased herself and destroyed his respect, longing the while feverishly to be free of

his reproachful presence. He, blanched and voice-
less, was scarcely cognizant he still was with her.
She yearned for him to go away. On the gravel
behind them one of the bigger girls whispered to
another, and the other giggled.

She made a slight movement, and he responded
with something impossible to catch. She did not
offer her hand; she did not immediately pity him.
Had a stranger told him this thing of her, she
would have pitied and understood; told him by
herself, she understood only that she was being
despised. They separated with a mechanical adieu,
quietly and slowly. The two girls, who watched
them with precocious eagerness, debated their
relationship.

The road lay before him long and bare, and he
took it lethargically. He continued to hear her
words, 'There used to be another man,' but he did
not know he heard them—he did not actively
pursue any train of thought. It was only in
momentary intervals that he became aware that

he was thinking. The sense of there being something numbed within him still endured, and as yet his sensation was more of stupor than of pain.

'There used to be another man!' The sentence rung in his ears, and as he went along he awoke to it, the persistence of it touched him; and he began repeating it—mentally, difficultly, trying to spur his mind into comprehension of it, and take it in. He did not suffer acutely even then. There was nothing acute in his feelings whatever. He found it hard to realize, albeit he did not doubt. She was what she had said she was; he knew it. But he could not see her so; he could not imagine her the woman she had said she used to be. He saw her always as she had been to him, composed and self-contained. The demeanour had been a mask, yet it clung to his likeness of her, obscuring the true identity from him still. He strove to conceive her in her past life, contemning himself because he could not; he wanted to remember he had been loving a disguise; he wanted to obliterate it. The fact of its having been a disguise all the time, and never she, was so hard to grasp. He tried to look upon her laughing in dishonour, but the picture would not live; it appeared unnatural. It was the inception of his agony: the feeling he had known her so very little that it was her real self which seemed the impossible.

And that other man had known it all — seen every mood of her, learned her in every phase!

'Mary!' he muttered; and was lost in the consciousness that actually he had never known Mary.

He perceived that the man was moving through his thoughts as a dark man, short and suave, and he wondered how the fancy had arisen. Vaguely he commenced to wonder what he had been like indeed. It was too soon to question who he was; he wondered only what he looked like, in a dim mental searching for the presence to connect her with. Grown cognizant of the impression, however, it vanished, and sudden recollections came to him of men he was accustomed to meet.

18—2

The manner and the mien of those riveted his attention. It was not by any volition of his own that he considered them; the personalities were insistent. He did not suppose any one of them had been her lover; he knew it was chimerical to view any one of them as such; but his brain had been groping for a man, and these familiar men obtruded themselves vividly. The lurking horror of her impurity materialized, so that the sweat burst out on him. The significance of what he had heard flared red upon his vision. In the flood and grip of that hideous conception masculinity looked loathsome to him, and he shuddered to associate it with her image. To think it had pleased her to lend herself for the toy of a man's leisure, that some man had been free to make her the boast of his conceit, twisted his heart-strings.

The solidity of the hospital confronted him on the slope he had begun to mount. Beneath him stretched the herbage of cottage gardens somnolent

in Sabbath calm. Out of the silence came the quick
yapping of a shop-boy's dog, the shrillness of a
shop-boy's whistle. They were the only sounds.
Then he went in.

That evening Miss Brettan told Mrs. Kincaid she
wished to leave her.

The old lady received the announcement without
any mark of surprise.

' You know your own mind best,' she said medi-
tatively ; ' but I am sorry you are going—very
sorry.'

' Yes,' said Mary; ' I must go. I am sorry to
leave you, too, but I can't help myself. I——'

' I used to think you would stop with me always;
we got on together so well.'

' You have been more than kind to me from the
very first day. I shall never forget how kind you
have been ! If it were only possible !—but it
isn't. I——'

Once more the pronoun was the stumbling-block
on delicate ground.

'I can't stop!' she added thickly; 'I hope you will be luckier with your next companion!'

'I shan't have another,' answered Mrs. Kincaid; 'changes upset me! New things are odious, I think! A new companion would be worse than new boots. And you must go when it suits you best, you know, since you have to go at all; don't stay on to give me time to make fresh arrangements; I have none to make. Study your own convenience exactly.'

'Then, this week?'

'Yes, very well; let it be this week.'

They said no more, and the subject dropped until the following afternoon, when Mrs. Kincaid broached it abruptly.

'What are you going to do, Miss Brettan?' she inquired. 'Have you anything else in view?'

'No,' replied Miss Brettan hesitatingly; 'not yet.'

The suppression of her motive made plain speaking difficult to both.

'I have no doubt, though,' she added, 'that I shall be all right.'

'What a pity it is! What a pity it is, to be sure!'

'Oh, you mustn't grieve about me!' she exclaimed; 'it isn't worth that! *I'm* not worth it! You know—you know, so many women have to make a living in the world; and they do make it, somehow; it's only one more!'

'And so many women find they can't! Tell me, *must* you go? Are you quite sure you're not exaggerating the necessity? I don't ask you your reasons. I never meddle in people's private affairs. But are you sure you aren't looking on anything in a false light, and going to extremes?'

'Oh!' responded Mary, carried into sudden candour, 'do you suppose I do not shiver at the prospect? Do you suppose it attracts me? I'm not a girl; I'm not quixotic; I *can't* stop here!'

The elder woman sighed.

'Why couldn't you care for such a good

fellow as my son?' she thought. 'Then there
would have been none of this bother for any
of us!'

'I hope you'll be fortunate,' she said gently.
'Anything I can do to help you of course I will.'

'Thank you!' said Mary.

'I mean, you mustn't scruple to refer to me; it's
your only chance. Without any references——'

'Yes, I know too well how indispensable they
are; but——'

'You have been here two years. I shall say I
should have liked it to remain your home.'

'Thank you,' said Mary again; but she was by
no means certain whether she could honestly avail
herself of this recommendation given in ignorance
of the truth. It was precisely the matter she had
been revolving in her mind. The doctor might
forbid its being accorded if she attempted to do so,
and she was loath to be indebted for testimony from
the mother which the son would know to be un-
deserved, whether he proclaimed her unworthiness

or no : she wanted her renunciation to be complete.
And yet, without this source of aid—— She
trembled.   How speedily the few pounds in her
possession would vanish ! how soon there would be
a revival of her past experience, with all its fright-
fulness and squalor ! In imagination she was
already footsore, adrift amid the heartless bustle
of the London streets.

'Mrs. Kincaid !' she cried. A passionate impulse
seized her to declare everything.   If she had
been seventeen, she would have knelt at the old
woman's feet ; for it is not so much the vehemence of our moods that diminishes with time
as the power of restraint which increases. 'Mrs.
Kincaid ! you must know — you must guess
why——'

'I know nothing,' said the old woman quickly ;
'I do not guess !' The colour sank from her face,
and Mary had never heard her speak with so much
energy. 'My son shall tell me—I have a son—I
will not hear from you !'

'I beg your pardon,' said Mary; and they were silent.

The same evening Mrs. Kincaid sent a message to the hospital, asking the doctor to come round to her.

There had been no intimation of this intention of hers, and her companion witnessed her instructions to the servant with a little shock. She apprehended, however, that they were delivered in her presence of design, and when it became possible for him to arrive she withdrew.

He came with misgivings and with relief. The last twenty-four hours had inclined him to the state of tension in which the unexpected is always the portentous, but in which one waits, nevertheless, for something unlooked-for to occur. He did not know what he dreaded to hear, but the summons alarmed him, even while he welcomed it for permitting him to go to the house.

He threw a rapid glance round the parlour, and

replied to his mother's greeting with quick inter-
rogation.

'What has happened?'

'Nothing of grave importance has happened. I
want to speak to you.'

'I was afraid something was the matter,' he
said, more easily. 'What is it?'

He took the seat opposite to her, and she was
dismayed to observe the alteration in him. She
contemplated him a few seconds irresolutely.

'Philip,' she said, 'this afternoon Miss Brettan
was anxious to tell me something; she wanted to
make me her confidant. And I would not listen
to her.'

'Oh!' he said. 'And you would not listen to
her?'

'No, I would not listen to her. I said, "My son
shall tell me, or I will not hear." This afternoon
I had no more idea of sending to you than you had
of coming. But I have been thinking it over. She

is in your mother's house, and she is the woman you love. You do love her, Philip?'

'I asked her to be my wife,' he answered simply.

'I thought so. And she has refused you?'

'Yes, she refused me. If I have not told you earlier, it was because she refused me. To have spoken of it would have been to give pain—needless pain—to you and to her.'

Mrs. Kincaid considered.

'You are quite right,' she admitted; 'your mistake was to suppose I should not see it for myself.' She turned her eyes from him, and looked ostentatiously in another direction. 'Now,' she added, 'she is going away! Perhaps you already knew, but——'

'No,' he replied, 'I did not know. I thought it likely, but I did not know. I understand why it was you sent for me.'

He got up and went across to her, and kissed her on the brow.

'I understand why you sent for me,' he repeated.

'What a tender little mother it is; and to lose her companion, too!'

Where he leant beside her over her chair, she could not see how white his face had grown.

'Are we going to let her go, Phil?'

He stroked her hand.

'I am afraid we must let her go, mother, since she does not wish to stop.'

'You do not mean to interfere, then? You won't do anything to prevent it?'

'I am not able to prevent it,' he rejoined coldly. 'I have not the authority.'

'Indeed!' murmured Mrs. Kincaid. 'It seems I might have spared my pains.'

'No,' said her son; 'your pains were well taken. I am very glad you have spoken to me— or, rather, I am very glad to have spoken to you— for you know now I meant no wrong by my silence.'

'But—but, Philip——'

'But Miss Brettan must go, mother, because she wishes it.'

'I do not understand you,' exclaimed Mrs. Kincaid, bewildered. 'I never thought you would care for any woman at all; you never struck me as the sort of man, somehow; but now that you do care, you can't surely mean you think it right for the woman to leave the only place where she has any friends, and go out into the world by herself! Don't you say you are in love with her?'

'I asked Miss Brettan to marry me,' he answered. 'Since you put the question, I do think it right for her to leave the place; I think every woman would wish to leave under the circumstances. I consider it would be indelicate to stay her.'

'Your sense of delicacy is very acute for a lover,' said the old lady grimly; 'much too fine a thing to be comfortable. And I'll tell you what is greater still—your pride. Don't imagine you take me in by your pretended calmness for a moment; look behind you in the glass, and ask yourself if it's likely.'

He had moved apart from her, and now was

lounging on the hearth : but he did not attempt to follow her advice, nor did he deny the implication.

'I look pretty bad,' he allowed, 'I know. But you are quite mistaken, for all that ; my pride has nothing to do with it.'

'You are making yourself ill at the prospect of losing her, and yet you won't—— Not but what she must be mad to reject you, certainly ! I am not standing up for her, don't think it ! I don't say I wanted to see you fond of her ; I should have preferred to see you marry someone who would have been of use to you, and helped you in your career. You might have done a great deal better, and I am sure I understand that you should have a proper pride in the matter, and object to begging her to remain. But, after all, if you do find so much in this particular woman that you are going to be miserable without her, why, *I* can say something to induce her to stop.'

'To the woman you would prefer me not to

marry !' he said wearily. 'But you must not do it, mother.'

'I do want to see you marry her, Philip; I want to see you happy. You don't follow me a bit. Since the dread of her loss can make you look like that, you mustn't lose her; that's what I say.'

'I *have* lost her,' he returned; 'I follow you very well. You think I might have married a princess, and you would have viewed that with a little pang too. You would give me to Miss Brettan with a big pang, but you would give me to her because you think I want her.'

'That is it—not a very big pang, either; I know every man is the best judge of his own life. Indeed, it ought not to be a pang at all; I don't think it *is* a pang, only a tiny—— Her son's sweetheart is always the mother's rival just at first, Phil; and I suppose it's always the mother's fault. But one day, when you're married to Mary, and a boy of your own falls in love with a strange girl, your wife will tell you how *she* feels. She'll explain it

to you better than I can, and then you'll know how
your mother felt, and it won't seem so unnatural.'

'Oh,' he said, 'hush! Don't! I shall never be
married to Mary.'

'Yes,' she declared, 'you will. When you say
that, you're not the "best judge" any longer; it
isn't judgment, it's pique, and I'm not going to
have your life spoiled by pique and the want of
resolution. Phil, Phil, you're the last man in the
world I should have thought would allow a thing
he wanted to slip through his fingers. And a
woman—women always say "no," to begin with.
It's not the girls who are to be had for the asking
who make the best wives; the ones who are hardest
to win are generally the worthiest to hold. Don't
accept her answer, Phil! I'll persuade her to stay
on, and at first you needn't come very often—I
won't mind any more, I shall know what it means
—and when you do come, I'll help you and tell you
what to do. She *shall* get fond of you; you *shall*
have the woman you want—I promise her to you!'

'Mother,' he said—the pallor had touched his lips—'for pity's sake don't say that! Don't go on talking of what can't be. It is no misunderstanding to be made up; it isn't any courtship to be aided. I tell you you can no more give me Mary Brettan for my wife than you can give my childhood back to me out of eternity.'

'And I tell you I will,' she averred. ' "Faint-heart"—you know what the proverb says! But you shall have your "fair lady" for all that; yes, instead of—you remember what we used to say to you when you were a little boy: "There's a monkey up your back, Phil!"—you shall have your fair lady instead of the monkey that's up your back! It's a full-grown monkey to-night, so that you're much too obstinate to listen to reason. By-and-by you will own you were wrong. She is suited to you; the more I think about it, the more convinced I am she would make you comfortable. You might have thrown yourself away on some flighty girl without a thought beyond her hats and

frocks ! And she is interested in your profession,
you have always been able to talk to her about it ;
she understands these things better than I do.'

'Listen to me,' exclaimed Kincaid with repressed
passion, 'listen to me, and remember what you
said just now, that I am a man—to judge for
myself ! You must not ask Miss Brettan to stay,
and you are not to think it is her going makes me
unhappy. My hope is over. Between her and me
there would never be any marriage if she remained
for years. Everything was said, and it was
answered, and it is done.'

He bit the end from a cigar, and smoked a little
before he spoke any more. When he did speak, his
tones were quite under control ; anyone from whom
his countenance was hidden would have pronounced
the words stronger than the feeling that dictated
them.

' Something else : after to-night don't talk to me
about her. I don't want to hear ; it is not pleasant
to me. If you want to prove your affection, prove

it by that.   While she remains, I cannot see you; when she is gone let it be, in our talks together, as if she had never been.'

The aspect of the man showed of what a tremendous strain this affected calmness was the outcome.   Indeed, the deliberateness of the utterance, even more than the utterance itself, hushed his listener into a conviction of his sincerity, which was disquieting because she found it so inexplicable. She smoothed the folds of her gown; casting at him, from time to time, glances full of wistfulness and pity, and at last she said, in the voice of a person who resigns herself to bewilderment:

'Well, of course I will do as you wish.   But you have both very queer notions of what is right, that is certain; help seems equally repugnant to the pair of you.'

'Why do you say that?' inquired the doctor. 'What help has Miss Brettan declined?'

'She was reluctant to refer anybody to me, I thought, when I chanced to mention the matter

to-day. But I suppose that was another instance
of delicacy that is over my head.'

' The reference? Do you mean she will not use
it ?'

' She gave me the idea of being very doubtful of
doing so. I said : " Without any references, what
on earth will become of you?" And she replied :
" Yes, she understood that; but——" But something; I forget exactly what it was now !'

' But that is insane !' he said imperatively.
' She is helpless without it. She has been your
" companion," and you have had no fault to find
with her : you can conscientiously declare as much.'

He rose, and shook his coat clear of the ash
which had fallen in a lump from the cigar.

' Nothing that has passed between Miss Brettan
and me can affect her right to your testimony to
the two years she has lived with you,' he added.
' I should like her to know I said so.'

' I will tell her,' affirmed his mother. ' What
are you going to do ?'

'It is getting late! . . . By the way, there is another thing: it will be a long while before she finds herself a home at the best; she mustn't think I have anything to do with it, but I want her to take some money before she goes, to keep her from distress. . . . Where did I leave my hat?'

'You want me to persuade her to take some money, as if it came from me?'

'Yes, as if it were from you—fifty pounds—to keep her from distress. . . . Did I hang it up outside?'

His mother went across to him, and put her arms about his neck. 'Can you spare so much, Philip?'

'I have been putting by,' he said, 'for some time.'

CHAPTER XI.

UNACQUAINTED with Kincaid's dictum, Mary spent the evening in grave anxiety. The formless future before her, if she declined to avail herself of his mother's recommendation, was a terror she could not banish, and she was unable to evolve any definite line of action out of the chaos on which to sustain a hope.

She sank later into a troubled sleep, from which she awoke suddenly with a startled sense of something having happened. After a few seconds, the impression was verified by a repetition of the cause. The hollow jangling of a bell broke the silence of the house, and nervous investigation proved it to be a summons to the old lady's room.

Mrs. Kincaid explained that she was feeling very unwell—an explanation that was corroborated by her voice—and, kindling a light, Mary was surprised to perceive she was shivering violently.

'I can't stop it; and I am so cold. I don't know what it is; I feel as if cold water were running down my back.'

Her companion looked at her quickly. 'We will put some more blankets on the bed,' she answered; 'wait a minute while I run upstairs.'

She returned with the clothes from her own, and piled them upon the quilt.

'You will be warmer presently,' she said; 'you must have taken a slight chill.'

Mrs. Kincaid lay mute awhile.

'I have such a pain!' she murmured. 'How could I have taken a chill?'

'Where is your pain?'

'In my side—a sharp, stabbing pain.'

The servant now appeared at the door, alarmed by the disturbance, and Mary told her to bring some coals, and then to dress herself as promptly as she could.

'Is there any linseed?—or oatmeal will do. I must make Mrs. Kincaid a poultice.'

'I'll see, miss. There's some linseed, I think, but——'

'Fetch it, please,' said Mary, 'and a kettle. We'll light the fire at once, and then I can make it up here.'

The old lady moaned and shivered by turns, and a little difficulty was experienced in getting the fire to burn. Mary attempted to draw the flicker into a blaze by the aid of a newspaper, while the servant advanced theories on the subject of the stove, affirming that, in her time at least, it had never been used.

When a glow had been obtained at length, and it was possible for the poultice to be applied, Miss Brettan sent her down for a hot-water bottle and the whisky.

'You will be so comfortable directly, you won't

know what to make of it!' she said brightly to the
invalid. 'Something warm to drink, and the hot
flannel to your feet—you'll feel a different being!'

'So cold I am, it's bitter—and the pain! I can't
think what it can be!'

'Let me put this on for you, then; it's all ready.
It won't—is that it?—there!—how's that?'

'Oh!' faltered Mrs. Kincaid, 'oh, thank you!
Ah! you do it very nicely!'

'See!' said Mary, her fingers busy, 'and here
we have the rest of the luxuries! Give me the
tumbler, Ellen, and we'll do that first.' She
mixed the stimulant, and carried it to the bedside.
'Just raise your head!' she murmured; 'I'll
hold the glass for you, so that you won't have to
sit up. Take this, now, and Ellen will get the
bottle ready while you're sipping it.'

'There isn't much in the kettle, miss,' said
Ellen. 'I don't——'

'Use what there is, and fill it up again; and
then see if you can find me any brown paper.'

In quest of the brown paper, Ellen was absent some time, and, having set down the empty tumbler and arranged the clothing about the recumbent figure more tidily, Miss Brettan proceeded to search for the requisite herself.

She found a sheet lining one of the drawers she opened, and, shifting it from beneath the handkerchiefs and cuffs, rolled it into a tube, which she affixed to the spout of the kettle to direct the steam into the room. She had not long done this when the girl returned disconsolate to say there was not such a thing in the house. Mary joined her on the stairs. No parcel such as they used brown paper for had been sent home lately, she averred. There was the paper the sugar came in, and the tea; but that was blue paper, and she could not find any of it, besides. ‘Are you going to sit in there all night, miss?’

‘Speak lower! Yes, I shall sit up. What time is it?’ The servant said it was just on half-past four, which had astonished her a good deal when she had learnt it by the kitchen clock, as she had supposed it to be about one at the latest. ' I want you to go and fetch the doctor, Ellen; I am afraid Mrs. Kincaid is going to be ill.'

' Now at once, miss ?'

' Yes, at once. Tell him his mother is unwell, and it would be better for him to see her. Bring him back with you. You aren't frightened to go out; it must be getting light?'

They drew up the blind of the landing window, and saw daylight creeping over the next door yard.

' Frightened ! not me ! And if I was I'd run an errand for you, miss ! Do you think she's going to be very bad ?'

' I don't know; I can't tell. Hurry, Ellen, there's a good girl ! get back as quickly as you can !'

A deep flush had overspread the face upon the pillows. The eyes yearned, and, an agonized expression, as Miss Brettan took her seat by the curtains again, strengthened her belief in the gravity of the seizure, which she dreaded might be the commencement of inflammation of the lungs. Three-quarters of an hour must be allowed for Kincaid to arrive, and, conscious she could now do nothing but wait, the time lagged fearfully. The silence, banished at the earlier pealing of the bell, had regained its dynasty, and once more a wide hush settled upon the house, indicated by the occasional clicking of a cinder on the fender. At intervals the sick woman uttered a tremulous sigh, and met Mary's gaze with a look of appeal, as if she recognised in her presence a kind of protective sympathy; but she had ceased to complain, and the watcher abstained from any active demonstration. In the globe beside the mirror the gas flared brightly, and this, coupled with the heat of the fire, filled the room with a moist radiance against which the narrow line of dawn above the window-sill grew slowly more defined. The advent had been long expected, when sharp footfalls on the pavement, ringing momentarily louder, smote

Mary's ear at last, and, forgetting Kincaid had his own key, she sprang up to let him in. The hall-door swung back, and she paused with her hand on the banisters. He came swiftly forward, and passed her with a hurried salutation on the stairs.

There was no anxiety, however, visible on the countenance with which he approached the bed. A little genial concern showed merely, such as it had worn when he had been told his mother had neuralgia, and the tone in which he addressed her seemed, by its matter-of-fact cheerfulness, to imply he understood and inwardly depreciated the patient's dread of detailing any serious symptoms. His questions were put encouragingly; when a reply was given he listened with the air of confidence confirmed.

' Am I very ill ?' she gasped.

' You *feel* very ill, I dare say, dear; but don't go persuading yourself you *are*, or that will be a real trouble !'

He had his fingers on her pulse as he spoke, and a smile on his lips. Yet he knew that her life was in danger. He had, in brief, mastered the art of acting on the noblest stage—the acting of a clever physician in a sick-room.

Mary stood on the threshold watching him.

'Who put that funnel to the kettle?' he inquired, without turning. He had not appeared to notice it.

'I did,' she answered. 'Is it to remain?'

'Yes; leave it.'

He signed to her she was to go below, and after a few minutes followed her into the parlour.

'Give me a pen and ink, Miss Brettan, please.'

'They are on the table,' she said, 'by the blotting-pad.'

He sat down and wrote hastily, rising with the paper held out.

'Where is Ellen?'

'She is here, waiting to take the prescription.'

A trace of surprise escaped his stiffness.   Then
he said curtly :

'You are thoughtful.   Was it you who put on
that poultice ?'

The tone of her affirmative was as distant as his.

'We did what we could until you arrived; *I* put
on the poultice.   Did I do right ?'

'Quite right.   It was the way it was put on that
made me ask.'

With that expression of approval he left her,
returning to his mother, and until the girl came
back from the chemist's Mary remained where she
was.   She then thought of attempting to complete
her toilette, but, unaware from minute to minute
when she might be called, was forced to abandon
the notion, and occupied herself by righting the
disorder of the room.   She had thrown on a
loosely-fitting morning dress of cashmere, one of
the first things she had made herself after her instalment, and, though she had snatched an instant
in the meanwhile to immerse her face in water,

had been able to do but little to her hair, the coil
of which still retained much of the scattered soft-
ness of the night. It was now possible to rectify
this, at least, and Ellen brought her the necessary
pins. She stood on the hearth before the looking-
glass, shaking the mass of hair about her
shoulders, and then with uplifted arms winding
it deftly upon her head. The supple femininity of
the attitude, so suggestive of recent rising, had,
with the earliness of the sunshine that tinged the
parlour, a certain harmony, and when Kincaid re-
entered and found her so, he could not but be
sensible of the impression, albeit he was indisposed
to dwell upon it.

As he came in she looked round quickly :

' How is Mrs. Kincaid, doctor ?'

' I am very uneasy about her. I am going back
to the hospital now to arrange to stay here.'

' What do you think has caused it ?'

' I am afraid she got damp and cold in the
garden on Sunday.'

' And it has gone to the lungs ?'

' It has affected the left lung, yes.'

She dropped the last pin, and as she stooped for it the swirl of the gown displayed a bare instep.

' I can help to nurse her, unless you prefer to send someone else ?'

' You will do very well, I think,' he answered ; and he proceeded to give her some instructions.

She fulfilled these instructions with a capability he found astonishing, though there was little astonishing in her competence, in fact. Before the day had worn through he perceived that, however her training had been acquired, he possessed in her a coadjutrix reliable and adroit, and the unexplained ability continued to amaze him after the discovery was made. She was, to herself, once more within her native province, but to him it was as if she had become suddenly voluble in a foreign tongue. He had no inclination to meditate upon her skill—to meditate about her at all was the last thing he desired now—but there were moments when her performance of some duty supplied fresh food for wonder notwithstanding, and he noted her dexterity with curious eyes. He had, though, refrained from any further commendation, the gratitude he might have spoken being checked by the aloofness of her manner; and, in the closer association consequent upon the illness, the formality that had sprung up between them suffered no decrease. It became, indeed, permanent in the contact which both would have shunned.

After the one opportunity, during which she had left the choice to him, she had afforded him no chance to resume their earlier relations had he wished it, and the studied politeness of her address was a persistent reminder that she directed herself to him in his medical capacity alone. In her own mind she held the present the least exacting conditions attainable, since the distastefulness of renewed intercourse was not to be avoided altogether; but she in nowise exonerated him for imposing them, and she considered that by having done so he had

20—2

made her a singularly ungracious return for the humiliation of her avowal. She sustained the note he had struck; the key was in a degree congenial to her. But she resented while she concurred, and even more than to her judgment her acquiescence was attributable to her pride.

On the day following there were recurrences of pain, but on Wednesday this subsided, though the temperature remained high. Mary observed that Kincaid's anxiety was, if anything, keener than it had been, and by degrees a latent admiration began to mingle with her bitterness. In the atmosphere of the sick-room the man and the woman were equally new to each other, and up to a certain point he was as great a surprise to her as she was to him. She saw him now professionally for the first time, and she recognised his resources, his despatch, with an appreciation quickened by experience. The visitor she had known lounging, loose-limbed and conversational, in an armchair had disappeared; the suppliant for a tenderness

she did not feel had become an authority whom she
obeyed. Here, like this, the man was a power, and
the change which came over him seemed a physical
one. His figure was braced, his movements had a
resolution and a vigour that gave him another per-
sonality. He even awed her slightly. She thought
he must look sterner to all the world in the exercise
of his vocation, but she thought also everyone in the
world would approve the difference.

The confidence he inspired in the beholder was
so strong that on Thursday, when he told her he
intended to have a consultation, she heard him with
a certain shock.

'You think it advisable ?'

'I fear the worst, Miss Brettan ; I can't neglect
any chance.'

She held some violets in her hands—it was her
custom to brighten the outlook from the bed with
fresh flowers every morning—and for an appreciable
space her acutest consciousness was of the faint
scent stealing up into her face.

'Do you mean she won't recover?' she said at last thickly.

'God grant my opinion's wrong!' he replied. 'Will you ask the girl to take the wire for me?'

It was to a physician in the county town he had decided to telegraph, one whose prestige was gradually widening, and of the class whose reputations have been built on something trustier than a cultivated eccentricity of manner and a chance summons to the couch of a notability. Mary had heard the name before, and she strove to persuade herself another view of the case might prove more promising. The day which had opened so gloomily, however, offered during the succeeding hours small food for faith. Towards noon the sufferer became abruptly restless, and the united efforts of doctor and nurse were required to soothe her. She was fired by a passionate longing to get up, and pleaded piteously for permission. To walk about a little while was her one appeal, and the strenuousness with which she urged the entreaty was rendered

more pathetic by her obvious belief that they
refused her because they failed to comprehend
the violence of the desire. She endeavoured with
failing energy to make it known, and, at length
prevailed upon to desist, lay back with a look in
her eyes which was a lamentation of her helplessness. Later slight delirium intervened, and she
rambled in confused phrases of her son and her
companion—his courtship and Mary's indifference.
The man and the woman sat on either side of her,
but their gaze no longer met. At the first reference
to his attachment the latter had started painfully,
but now by a strong effort her nervousness had
been suppressed, and from time to time she moved
to wipe the fevered lips and brow with a semblance
of self-possession. While the day-beams waned the
disjointed sentences grew rarer. The doctor went
below, and silence, save for the deep breathing, fell
again, until suddenly, as dusk gathered, the words
'I feel much better' were uttered in a tone of
restored tranquillity. Wheeling round, Mary saw

that her ears had not deceived her. The declaration was repeated with a feeble smile. The features had gained a touch of the cheerfulness which had been so remarkable in the voice. The eyes soon afterwards closed in what appeared to be slumber. Kincaid had not come up when this occurred.

He was striding backwards and forwards, his arms locked across his breast. As Mary ran in he turned sharply, with lifted head.

'She feels much better,' she exclaimed; 'she has fallen asleep.'

He stood still, in the middle of the room, never speaking.

'She feels m—— Oh!' She shrank back with a stifled cry, staring at him in the twilight. 'I have never seen—I—— Is it *that?*'

'Hush!' he said, scarcely above a whisper. And she understood what she had told him was the presage of death.

After this, both knew it to be but a matter of time. The arrival of the physician served merely to confirm despondency. He pronounced the case hopeless, and, reluctantly accepting a fee to reimburse the expenses of the journey, bade Kincaid farewell with an expression of sympathy in which an allusion to their profession was not inaptly blended.

'I wish you could have associated our meeting with happier circumstances,' he said. 'If anything can mitigate your sorrow, it must be the reflection that you were able to do everything that could be done yourself.'

A page with a message of inquiry came up the steps as he left; indeed, such messages had been delivered daily. But on Saturday, when the baker's man brought the bread to Laburnum Lodge, he found the blinds drawn down; and within a few minutes of his handing the loaf to the weeping servant through the scullery window, the news was circulating through Westport that Mrs. Kincaid had died unconscious at seven that morning.

While the baker's man derived this intelligence from the housemaid, Mary was behind the lowered blinds on the first floor, crying. She had just descended from her own apartment, whither she had retired soon after the end. She had seen how deeply Philip was affected, and had withdrawn from him as speedily as might be. He had not shed tears—he was not the man to break down had he been alone—but that he was strongly moved was evident by the quivering muscles of his mouth ; and the drawn face of which she had had a glimpse kept recurring to her vividly.

He came in while she sat there. He was very pale, but now his countenance was under control again.

She rose, and advanced towards him irresolutely. 'I am so sorry! She was a very kind friend to me.'

He put out his hand. For the first time since she had met him after posting the note hers lay in it.

'Thank you,' he said. 'Thank you, too, for all you did for her; I shall always remember it gratefully, Miss Brettan.'

He seemed on the point of adding something, but checked himself, and presently made reference to the arrangements which must be seen to. That night he reoccupied his quarters in the hospital, nor did they come together excepting in odd minutes during the day. She, however, found space to mention that she purposed remaining until the funeral, and to this announcement he bowed, though he refrained from framing any inquiry as to her plans for afterwards. Indeed, 'plans' would have been a curious misnomer for the thoughts in her brain. The question she had earlier revolved had been settled effectually by the death, and now that all possibility of recommendation had been removed, her plight admitted of nothing but conjecture.

In her solitude in the house of mourning, unbroken save for interruptions which emphasized

the ghastliness of what had happened, or by some
colloquy with the red-eyed servant, she passed her
hours lethargic and weary. The week of suspense
and insufficient rest had tired her out, and she no
longer even sought to consider. Her mind drifted.
A fancy that often came to her was that it would
be a delightful thing to be far away, lying in a
cornfield in the hot sunshine, with a vault of blue
above her. The picture looked to her sweet, with
infinite peace. It was present with her more
frequently than the impending horrors of the
seething capital.

How much the week had held! what changes it
had seen! She sat musing on this next evening,
listening to the church bells, and remembering
that a Sunday ago the dead woman had been
beside her. Last Sunday there was still a prospect
of Westport continuing to be her home for years.
Last Sunday it was that in the churchyard she
had confessed her past. Only a week—how full,
how difficult to realize! She was half dozing

when she heard the hall-door unlocked, and Kincaid greeted her as she roused herself.

'Did I disturb you ? were you asleep?'

'No; I was thinking, that is all.'

He sighed, and dropped into the opposite chair. She noted his harassed aspect, and pitied him. The Sunday previous she had not been sensible of any pity at all. She understood his loss of his mother; the loss of his faith had represented much less to her, being a faith on which she personally had set small store.

'There is plenty to think of!' he said wearily.

'You haven't seen Ellen, doctor, have you? She has been asking for you.'

'Has she? what does she want?'

'She is anxious to know how long she will be retained. Her sister is in service somewhere, and the family want a parlourmaid on the first of the month. I am sorry to bother you with trifles now, but she asked me to speak to you.'

'I must talk to her. Of course the house will

be sold off; there is no one to keep it on for. How fagged you look! are you taking proper care of yourself again?'

'Oh yes; it is just the reaction, nothing but what will soon pass.'

'You did not have the relief you ought to have had; you worked like two people.'

He paused, and his gaze dwelt on her inquiringly. She read the inquiry with such clearness that when he spoke the words seemed but an echo of the pause.

'How did you know so much?' he said.

'After I lost my father I was nurse in the Yaughton Hospital for several years.'

The answer was direct, but it was brief. Half a dozen queries sprang to his lips in the ensuing seconds, and were in turn repressed. Her past was her own; he confined his questions to her future.

'And what do you propose to do now?'

'I am going to London.'

'Do you anticipate any obstacles to resuming your old occupation ?'

'I think you know that I have found obstacles.'

'I have no wish to force your confidence,' he said diffidently.

'I haven't my certificate.'

'You can refer to the matron.'

'I know I can; I will not. I told you two years ago there were persons I could refer to, and I would not do it.'

'May I ask your objection to referring to this one ?'

She was silent.

'Won't you tell me ?'

'I think you might understand,' she said in a very low voice. 'I went there after my father's death. I am not the woman who left the Yaughton Hospital.'

His eyes fell, and he stared abstractedly at the grate. When he raised them he saw that hers had closed. He looked at her lingeringly till they opened.

' Now that *she* is gone,' he exclaimed unsteadily,
' your position is a very difficult one! Have you
any prospect that you do not mention ?'

She shook her head.

' Is there anything you can suggest? Any way
out of the difficulty that occurs to you ? Believe
me——'

' No,' she said, ' I can see nothing that is practicable ; I——'

' Would you be willing to come on the nursing-
staff here? We are short-handed in the night
work. It is an opening, and it might lead to a
permanent appointment.'

Her heart began to beat rapidly; for an instant
she did not reply.

' It is very considerate of you, very generous ;
but I am afraid that would not do.'

' Why not ?'

' It would not do, because I should have left
Westport in any case—of my own accord.'

' You had the intention, I'm aware. But between

the manner of your leaving Westport if my mother had lived, and the way you would leave it now, there is a vast difference.'

'I must leave it, all the same.'

'Pardon me,' he said; 'I cannot permit you to do so. I would not permit any woman to go out into the world with the knowledge she went to meet certain distress. Your hospital experience appears to me to present a very natural solution to the dilemma. You could come on next week. If your reluctance is attributable to myself—hear me out, I must speak plainly—if you refuse because what has passed between us makes every further conversation a pain to you, you have only to re-collect that conversation between us in the hospital will necessarily be of the very briefest kind. All that *I* recollect is that I have asked you to be my wife, and you do not care for me—I am the man you have rejected. I wish, though, to be some-thing more serviceable : I wish to be your friend. In the hospital I shall have little chance, for there, to all intents and purposes, we shall be as much divided as if indeed you went to London. While the chance does exist I want to use it. I want to advise you strongly to adopt the course I propose. Acceptance, bear in mind, need in no way prevent you attempting to find a post elsewhere; it would, on the contrary, facilitate your obtaining one.'

Her hand had shaded her brow as she listened; now it sank slowly to her lap.

'I need hardly tell you I am grateful,' she said, in tones that struggled to be firm. 'Anyone must be grateful; to me the offer is very—is more than good.' Her composure broke down. 'I know what I must seem to you; you have heard nothing but the worst of me,' she exclaimed.

'I would hear nothing that it hurt you to say,' he answered; and for a minute neither of them said any more. There had been a gentleness in his last words that touched her keenly; the appeal in hers had stirred the soul of him. Neither spoke, but the man's breath rose eagerly, and the woman's head drooped lower and lower on her breast.

'Let me!' she said at last, in a whisper his pulses leaped to meet. 'It was there—when I was nurse. He was a patient. Before he left he asked me to marry him; I was to go to him in a few weeks. When I went he told me he was married already. Until then there had been no hint, not the faintest suspicion—I went to him, with the knowledge of them all, to be his wife.'

'Thank God!' said the other in his throat.

'She was — she had been on the streets; he had not seen her for years. He prayed to me, implored me—— Oh, I am not trying to exonerate myself! I am not trying to shift the sin on to him; but if the truest devotion of her life can plead for a woman, Heaven knows that plea was mine!'

'And at the end of the three years?'

'There was news of her death, and he married someone else.'

She got abruptly up, and moved to the window, looking out from behind the blind.

'I can't tell you how I feel for you,' he said huskily. 'I can't give you an idea how deeply, how earnestly I sympathize!'

'Don't say anything,' she murmured; 'you need not try: I think I understand to-night—you proved your sympathy while the claim on it was least.'

'And you will let me help you?'

The slender figure stood motionless; behind her the man was gripping the leather of his chair.

'If I may,' she said constrainedly, 'if I can go there like—as you—ah, if the past can all be buried, and there need be no reminder of what has been!'

'I will be everything you wish, everything that you would have me seem!'

He took a sudden step towards her. She turned, her eyes humid with tears, with thankfulness, with entreaty. He stopped short, drew back, and resumed his seat.

' Now, what were you saying about Ellen ?' he inquired.

And perhaps it was the plainest avowal he had ever made her of his love.

CHAPTER XII

So it happened that Mary Brettan did not leave Westport the next week, and that after a few months she was more than ever doubtful if she would leave it at all. The suggested vacancy on the permanent staff had occurred before then, and, once having accepted the post, there seemed no inducement to woo anxiety by resigning it.

At first the resumption of routine after years of indolence was irksome and exhausting. The six o'clock rising, the active duties commencing while she still felt tired, the absence of anything like privacy excepting in the two hours allotted to each nurse for leisure—all these things fretted her. The relief she derived from her escape into the open air

was itself alloyed by the knowledge that outdoor
exercise during one of the hours was compulsory.
Then, too, it was inevitable that a costume worn
once more should recall the emotions with which
she had laid aside her last; inevitable that she
should ask herself what the years had done for
her since last she stood within a hospital, and bade
it farewell with the belief she was never going to
enter one again. The evolution of fate which had
cast her back into her original surroundings accen-
tuated the failure of the interval. Her heart had
contracted when, directed to the strange apartment
above the wards, she beheld the print dress provided for her use lying limp upon a chair. An unutterable forlornness filled her soul as, proceeding
to put it on, she surveyed her reflection in the
narrow glass. Yet she grew accustomed to the
change, and the more easily for its being a revival.

The speed with which the sense of novelty wore
off indeed astonished her. Primarily dismaying,
and a continuous burden upon which she condoled

with herself every day, it was next as if she had
lost it one night in her sleep. She had forgotten
it until the lightness with which she was fulfilling
the work struck her with swift surprise. Little by
little a certain enjoyment in its performance was
even felt. She contemplated some impending task
with interest. She took her walk with zest in lieu
of relief. She returned to the doors exhilarated
instead of depressed. The Bohemian, the lady-
companion, had become a sick-nurse anew, and
because the primary groove of life is the one
which cuts the deepest lines, her existence rolled
along the recovered rut with smoothness. The
scenes between which it lay were not beautiful,
but they were familiar; the view it commanded
was monotonous, but she no longer sought to
travel.

Socially the conditions had been favoured by her
introduction. The position she had occupied in
Laburnum Lodge gave her a factitious value, and
gained her the friendliness of the matron, a func-

tionary who has the power to make the hospital-
nurse distinctly uncomfortable, and who has on
occasion been known (by the hospital-nurse) to use
it. It commended her also to the other nurses,
two of whom were gentlewomen, insomuch as it
promised an agreeable variety to conversation in
the sitting-room. She was by no means unconscious of the extent of her debt to Kincaid, and
her gratitude as time went on increased rather
than diminished. Certainly the environment was
conducive to a perception of his merits, more conducive even than had been the period of his
attendance at the villa. The king is nowhere so
attractive as at his court ; the preacher nowhere so
impressive as in the pulpit. Ashore the captain
may bore us, but we all like to smoke our cigars
with him on his ship. The poorest pretender
assumes importance in the circle of his adherents,
and poses with authority on some small platform,
if it be only his mother's hearthrug. Here where
the doctor was the guiding spirit, and Mary found

his praises upon every tongue, the glow of gratitude was fanned by the breath of popularity.
In fact, had he deliberately planned a means of
raising himself in her esteem, he could have de-
vised none better than this of placing her as
inmate of the miniature kingdom that he ruled.
In remembering he had wanted to marry her, she
was sensible one day of a thrill of pride : nothing
like regret, nothing like arrogance, but a momentary pride. She felt more dignity in the moment.

If he remembered it too, however, no word he
spoke evinced such recollection. The promise he
had made to her had been kept to the letter, and
the past was never alluded to between them. As
doctor and nurse their colloquies were brief and
practical. It was the demeanour he adopted
towards her from the date of her instalment which
added the first fuel to her thankfulness, and if,
withal, she was inclined to review his generosity
rather than to regard it, it was because he had
established the desired relations on so firm a

footing that she ceased to believe the pursuance of it cost him any pains. That she had held his love after the story of her shame she was aware; but that on reflection he could still want her for his wife she did not for an instant suppose, and she often thought that by degrees his attitude had become the one most natural to him.

By what a denial of nature, by what rigid self-restraint, the idea had been conveyed, nobody but the man himself could have told. No one else knew the bitterness of the suffering that had been endured to give her that feeling of right to remain; what impulses had been curbed and crushed back, that no scruples or misgivings should cross her peace. The circumstances under which they met now helped him much, or he would have failed despite his efforts, and to fail, he understood, would be to prove unworthy of her trust; it would be to see her go out from his life for ever. Still want her? So intensely, so devoutly did he want her, that, shadowed by sin as she was, she was

holier to him than any other woman upon earth—
fairer than any other gift at God's bestowal. He
would have taken her to his heart with as profound
a reverence as if no shame had ever touched her.
If all the world had been cognizant of her disgrace,
he would have triumphed to cry ' My wife !' in the
ears of all the world. A baser love might well
have thirsted for her too, but it would have had
its hours of hesitation. Kincaid's had none. No
flood of passion blinded his higher judgment and
urged him on ; no qualms of convention intervened
and gave him pause. It was with his higher
judgment that he prayed for her. His love burned
steadily, clearly. The situation lacked only one
essential for the ideal : the love of the penitent he
longed to raise. The complement was missing.
The fallen woman who had confessed her guilt, the
man's devotion that had withstood the test—these
were there. But the devotion was unreturned, the
constancy was not desired. He could only wait,
and try to hope ; wondering if her tenderness

would waken in the end, wondering how he would learn it if it did.

To break the word he had passed to her by pleading again was a thing he could only do in the belief that she would listen to him with happiness. If he misread her mind, and spoke too soon, he not merely committed a wrong—he destroyed the slender link there was between them, for he made it impossible for her to stay on. And yet, how to divine ? how, without speaking, to ascertain if she would hear him now with other feelings? What could be gathered from the deep gray eyes, the serious face, the slim-robed figure, as he some-times stood beside her, guarding his every look and schooling his voice? How could he tell if she cared for him unless he asked her ? how could he ask her unless he had reason to suppose she did ? The nature of their association seemed to him to impose an insurmountable barrier between them. In freer parlance a ray of the truth might be discernible, and when she had been here a year he determined to gain an opportunity of talking with her alone; to talk with her, if not on matters nearest to him, at least on topics less formal than those to which their conversation was limited in the ward.

Such an opportunity, however, did not lie to his hand. It was difficult to compass without betraying himself, and, in view of the present difficulties, he appeared to have had so many advantages earlier, that he marvelled he could have turned them to so little account. Their acquaintance at the villa during his mother's lifetime appeared to him, by comparison, to have afforded every facility which he was to-day denied, and he frequently recalled the period with passionate regret, thinking he had never appreciated it at its worth, while, indeed, he had only failed to benefit by it. The house was tenanted now by a lady with two children, and Mary often passed it, recalling the period also, albeit with a melancholy vaguer than his. One morning, when she went by, the

door was open—the children were coming out—and
·she had a glimpse of the hall.

They came down the steps, carrying spades and
pails, evidently bound for the beach, like herself.
The elder of them might have been nine, and,
belonging to the familiar house, there was a little
sad interest in watching them. She wondered, as
they preceded her along the pavement, which of
the rooms they slept in, and if the different furniture had altered the aspect of it much. She thought
she would like to speak to them when the sands
were gained, and then—— You know how, in
sauntering along a busy street, one suddenly sees
a single face, to the exclusion of all else, so that
it seems to smite the eyes, and the perspective
narrows to it ? Then she saw Seaton Carew !
Her heart rose into her throat, her gaze was
riveted on him; she could not withdraw it. They
were advancing towards each other, and he was
looking at her. She saw recognition flash across
his features, and turned her head. The people to

right and left swayed a little, and she had passed him. It had taken just fifteen seconds, but she could never remember what she was thinking of when she had seen him. The fifteen seconds had held more emotion for her than the last twelve months.

Her knees trembled. She supposed he must be at the theatre this week, but, when she noticed a playbill displayed outside the music-seller's, was afraid to examine it for fear he might be staring after her. She walked excitedly on. She was filled with a tremulous elation which she cared neither to define nor to acknowledge. She was conscious that it was fortunate she had quitted the hospital a few minutes earlier than usual, or she might have missed him. 'Missed' was the word of her reflection. She wondered where he was staying — in which streets the professional lodgings of Westport were. She felt suddenly strange in the town. She had been here three years, and she did not know — how odd! In turning a corner she saw another advertisement of the theatre, this time on a hoarding. The day was Monday, and the paper was still shiny with the bill-sticker's paste. She was screened from observation, and for a moment she paused before it, devouring the cast with a rapid glance. His wife's name did not appear, nor was it their own company; he was fulfilling an engagement in it. She hurried on again. The encounter had acted on her like a strong stimulant. Without knowing why, she was exhilarated. The air was sweeter, life was keener; she was anxious to reach the shore, and find herself in her favourite spot, and give herself up wholly to meditation.

And how little he had changed! Indeed, he seemed scarcely to have changed at all. He looked just as he used to do, though he must have gone through much since the night they parted. Ah, how could she forget that parting? how allow the sting of it to wax fainter? It was pitiful that one could feel things so intensely when they happened, and not be able to keep the intensity alive. The waste of sensation! The puerility of loving or hating, of mourning or rejoicing, so violently in life, when the progress of time, the interposition of irrelevant incident, would smear the passion that engrossed one into an occurrence that one recalled!

She sank on to the bench upon the slope of ragged grass that merged into the shingles and the sand. The sea, vague and unruffled, lay like a sheet of oil, veiled in mist saving for one bright patch on the horizon where it quivered luminously. She bent her eyes upon the sea, and saw the past. His voice struck her soul before she heard his footstep. 'Mary!' he said, and she knew that he had followed her.

She did not speak, she did not move. The blood surged into her temples, and left her body cold. She struggled for self-command; for the ability to conceal her agitation; for the power she yearned to gather of blighting him with the scorn she wanted to feel.

'Won't you speak to me?' he said. He came round to her side, and stood there, looking down at her. 'Won't you speak?' he repeated — 'a word?'

'I have nothing to say to you,' she murmured. 'I hoped that I might never see you any more.'

He waited awkwardly, kicking the soil with the point of his boot, his gaze wandering from her over the ocean—from the ocean back to her.

'I have often thought about you,' he said at last with a jerk—'do you believe that?'

She maintained a silence, and then made as if she would rise.

'Do you believe that I have thought about you?' he demanded quickly. 'Answer me!'

'It is nothing to me whether you have thought or not. I dare say you have been ashamed when you remembered your disgrace—what of it?'

'Yes,' he said, 'I have been ashamed. You were always too good for me; I ought never to have had anything to do with a woman like you.'

She had not risen; she was still in the position in which he had surprised her, and she was sensible now of a dull pain at the unexpectedness of his conclusion.

'Why have you followed me?' she said coldly. 'For what purpose?'

'Purpose! Why, I didn't know you were in the town; I hadn't an idea, and I saw you suddenly. I wanted to speak to you.'

'What is it you want to say?'

'Mary!'

'Yes; what do you want to say? I am not your friend; I am not your acquaintance: what have you got to speak to me about?'

'I meant,' he stammered—'I wanted to ask you if it was possible, if—if you could ever forgive the way I behaved to you.'

'Is that all?' she asked in a hard voice.

'How you have altered! Yes, I don't know that there's anything else.'

She did not reply, and he regarded her irresolutely.

' Can you ?'

' No,' she said. ' Why should I forgive you ?
Because time has gone by ? Is that any merit
of yours ? You treated me brutally, infamously.
The most that a woman can do for a man I did for
you ; the worst that a man can do to a woman you
did to me. You meet me accidentally, and expect
me to forgive it—you must be a great deal less
worldly-wise than you were three years ago.'

She turned to him for the first time since he had
joined her, and his eyes fell.

' I didn't expect,' he said ; ' I only asked. So
you're a nurse again, eh ?'

' Yes.'

He gave an impatient sigh, the sigh of a man
who realizes the discordancy of life, and imperfectly
resigns himself to it.

' We're both what we used to be, and we're both

older. Well, I'm the worse off of the two, if that's any consolation to you. A woman's always getting opportunities for new beginnings.'

She checked the retort that sprang to her lips, eager to glean some knowledge of his affairs, though she could not bring herself to put a question; and after a moment she rejoined indifferently:

'You got the chance you were so anxious for. I understood your marriage was all that was necessary to take you to London.'

'I was in London—didn't you hear?' He was startled into naturalness, the actor's naïve astonishment when he finds his movements are unknown to anyone. 'We had a season at the Boudoir, and opened with "The Cast of the Die." It was a frost; and then we put on a piece of Sargent's. That might have been worked into a success if there had been money enough left to run it at a loss for a few weeks, but there wasn't. The mistake was, not to have opened with it instead. And the capital was too small altogether for a

London show; the "exes" were awful! It would
have been better to have been satisfied with
management in the provinces if one had known
how things were going to turn out. Now it's the
provinces under somebody else's management—I
suppose you think I have been very rightly served?'

'I don't see that you're any worse off than you
used to be,' she observed.

'Don't you? You've no interest to see. I'm
a lot worse off, for I've a wife and child to
keep.'

'A child! You have a child?' she said.

'A boy. I don't grumble about that, though;
I'm fond of the kid, although I dare say you think
I can't be very fond of anyone. But — oh, I
don't know why I tell you about it—what do you
care?'

They were silent again. The sun, a disc in gray
heavens, smeared the vapour with a shaft of pale
rose, and on the water this was glorified and
enriched, so that the stain on the horizon had

turned a deep red. Nearer land, the sea, voluptuously still, and by comparison colourless, had yet some of the translucence of an opal, a thousand elusive subtleties of tint which gleamed between the streaks of darkness thrown upon its surface from the sky. A thin edge of foam unwound itself dreamily along the shore. A rowing-boat passed blackly across the crimsoned distance, gliding into the obscurity where sky and sea were one. To their right the shadowy form of a fishing-lugger loomed indistinctly through the mist. The languor of the scene had, in contemplation, something emotional in it, a quality that acted on the senses like music from a violin. She was stirred with a mournful pleasure that he was here—a pleasure of which the melancholy was a part. The delight of union stole through her, more exquisite for incompletion.

'It's nothing to you whether I do badly or well,' he said gloomily. And the dissonance of the complaint jarred her back to common-sense. 'Yet it isn't long ago that we—good Lord! how women can forget; now it's nothing to you!'

'Why should it be anything?' she exclaimed. 'How can you dare to remind me of what we used to be? "Forget!"—yes, I have prayed to forget! To forget I was ever foolish enough to put faith in your honour, and belief in your protestations; to forget I was ever debased enough to like you. I wish I could forget it; it's my punishment to remember. Not because I sinned—bad as it is, that's less—but because I sinned for *you!* If all the world knew what I had done, nobody could despise me for it as I despise myself, or understand how I despise myself. The only person who should is you, for you know what sort of man I did it for.'

'I was carried away by a temptation — by ambition. You make me out as vile as if it had been all deliberately planned. After you had gone——'

'After I had gone you married your manageress.

If you had been in love with her, even, I could make excuses for you; but you weren't: you were in love only with yourself. You deserted a woman for money. Your "temptation" was the meanèst, the most contemptible thing a man ever yielded to. "Ambition"? God knows I never stood between you and that! Your ambition was mine, as much my own as yours, something we halved between us. Has anybody else understood it and encouraged it so well? I longed for your success as fervently as you did; had you succeeded, I should have rejoiced as greatly. When you were disappointed, to whom did you come for consolation? But I could only give you sympathy; and she could give you power. And everything of mine *had* been given; you had had it. That was the main point.'

'Call me a villain, and be done—or a "man"! Will reproaches help either of us now?'

'Don't deceive yourself: there are noble men in the world! I tell you now, because at the time I

would say nothing you could regard as an appeal.
It only wanted that to complete my indignity—for
me to plead to you to change your mind !'

'I wish to Heaven you had done anything rather
than go, and that's the truth !'

'*I* don't; I am glad I went—glad, glad, glad !
The most awful thing I can imagine is to have
remained with you after I knew you for what you
are. The most awful thing for you as well : knowing that I knew, the sight of me would have
become a curse.'

'One mistake,' he muttered, 'one injustice, and
all the rest, all that came before, is blotted out;
you refuse to remember the sweetest years of both
of our lives !'

She gazed slowly round at him with lifted head,
and during a few seconds each looked in the
other's face, and tried to read the history of the
interval in it. Yes, he had altered, after all. The
eyes were older. Something had gone from him,
something of vivacity, of hope.

'Are you asking me to remember?' she said. 'You seem to forget for what purpose the injustice was done.'

'Mary, if you knew how wretched I am!'

'Ah,' she murmured half sadly, half wonderingly, 'what an egotist you always are! You meet me again—after the way we parted—and you begin by talking about yourself!'

He made a gesture—dramatic because it expressed the feeling he desired to convey so perfectly —and turned aside.

'May I question you?' he asked lamely the next minute. 'Will you answer?'

'What is it that you care to hear?'

'Are you at the hospital?'

'Yes.'

'For long? I mean, is it long since you came to Westport?'

'I have been here nearly all the time.'

'And do—how—is it comfortable?'

'Oh,' she said, with a movement she was unable

to repress, 'let us keep to you, if we must talk at all. You will find the words come easier.'

'Why will you be so cruel?' he exclaimed. 'It is you who are unjust now! If I am awkward, it is because you are so curt. You have all the right on your side, and I have the burden of the past on me. You asked me why I spoke to you: if you had been less to me than you were—if I had thought about you less than I have—I shouldn't have spoken. You might understand the position is a very hard one to me; I am wholly at your mercy, and you show me none.'

The hands in her lap trembled a little, and after a pause she said in a low voice:

'You expect more from me than is possible; I have suffered too much.'

'My trouble has been worse. Ah! don't smile like that: it has been far worse! You have at least had the solace of knowing you have been ill-used: I feel all the time that my bed is of my own making, and that I behaved like a blackguard. Whatever I have to put up with I deserve, I'm quite aware of it ; but the knowledge makes it all the beastlier. My life isn't idyllic, Mary ; if it weren't for the child— upon my soul ! the only moments I get rid of my worries are when I'm playing with the kid, or when I'm drunk.'

' Your marriage has not been happy !'

He shrugged his shoulders.

' We don't fight ; we don't throw the furniture at each other, and have the landlady up, like—what was their name?—the Whittacombes.   But we don't find the days too short to say all we've got to tell each other, she and I ; and—oh, you can't think what a dreadful thing it is to be in front of a woman all day long that you haven't got anything to say to—it's awful !   And she can't act, and she doesn't get engagements, and it makes her peevish. She might get " shopped " along with me for small parts—in fact, she did once or twice—but that doesn't satisfy her ; she wants to go on playing " lead," and now the money's gone she can't.

She thinks I mismanaged the damned money, and advised her badly. She hadn't been doing anything for a year until the spring, and then she went out with Laura Henderson to New York. Poor enough terms they are for America, but she'd been grumbling, so I believe she'd go on as an "extra" now rather than nothing, so long as I wasn't playing "lead" to another woman in the same crowd.'

She traced an imaginary pattern with her finger on the seat. He was still standing, and suddenly his face lighted up.

' There's Archie !' he said.

' Archie ?'

' The boy.'

A child of two years, in charge of a servant-girl, was at the gate of one of the cottages behind them.

' You take him about with you ?'

' He was left with some people in town ; I've just had him down, that's all. We finish on Saturday, and there's the sea : I thought two or three weeks of it would do him good. Will you—may he come over to you ?'

He held out his arms, and the child, released from the servant's clasp, toddled smilingly across the grass, a plump little body in pelisse and cape. The gaitered legs covered the ground slowly, and she watched his child running towards him for what seemed a long time before Carew caught him up.

'This is Archie,' he said diffidently; 'th s s he.'

'Oh,' she said, in constrained tones, 'this is he ?'

The man stood him on the bench with a pretence of carelessness that was ill done, and righted his hat quickly, as if afraid the action might savour of the ridiculous. The sight of him in this association had something infinitely strange to her—something that sharpened the sense of separation, and made the past appear intensely old and ended.

'Put him down,' she said ; 'he isn't comfortable.'

' Do you think he looks strong ?'

' I should say remarkably so. Why ?'

' I've wondered — I thought you'd know more about it than I do. Is Archie a good boy ?'

' Iss,' answered the child. ' Mama !'

' Don't talk nonsense—mama's over there !' He pointed to the sea. ' He talks very well for his age, as a rule ; now he's stupid.'

' Oh, let him be,' she said, looking at the baby-face with deep eyes ; ' he's shy, that's all.'

' Mama !' repeated the mite insistently, and laid a hand on her long cloak.

' The thumb is wrong,' she murmured after a pause in which the man and woman were both embarrassed ; ' see, it isn't in !'

She drew the tiny glove off, and put it on once more, taking the fragile fingers in her own, and parting with them slowly. A feeling complex and wonderful crept into her heart at the voice of Tony's child, a feeling of half-reluctant tenderness, coupled with an aching jealousy of the womanhood that had borne him one.

They made a group to which any glance would have reverted—a trio on whose connection any educated passer-by would have speculated without guessing it: the old-young man, who was obviously the father; the baby; and the thoughtful woman, whose dress proclaimed her to be a nurse. The dress, indeed, which was perhaps the group's most conspicuous feature, was not without its influence on Carew. It reminded him of the days of his and her first acquaintance, since which they had been together, and separated, and drifted into different channels. Having essayed matrimony as a means to an end, and proved it a *cul-de-sac*, he blamed the woman with whom he had blundered very ardently, and would have been gratified to dilate on his mistake to the other one, who was more than ever attractive because she no longer belonged to him. The length of veil which fell below her waist had, in his fancy, a cloistral suggestion which imparted to his allusions to their intimacy an additional fascination ; and Archie's presence had seldom occupied his attention so little. Yet he was fonder of this offshoot of himself than he had been of her even in the period which the dress recalled, and it was because she dimly understood the fact that the child touched her so nearly. Like almost every man in whom the cravings of ambition have survived the hope of their fulfilment, he dwelt a great deal on the future of his son ; longed to see his boy achieve the success which he had come to realize he would never attain himself, and lost in the interest of fatherhood some of the poignancy of failure. The desire to talk to her of these and many other things was strong in him, but she roused herself from reverie and said good-bye, as if on sudden impulse, just as he was meaning to speak.

'I shall see you again ?'

' I think not.'

Then he would have asked if they parted in peace, but her leave-taking was too abrupt even for him to formulate the inquiry.

CHAPTER XIII.

IT surprised him, and left him vaguely disappointed. To break off their interview thus sharply seemed to him motiveless and odd. He could suggest no explanation for it, and his gaze followed her receding figure with speculative regret. When she was out of sight he picked the child up, and, carrying him into the cottage parlour, sat down beside the open window, smoking and thinking of her.

It was a small room, poorly furnished, and, fretted by its limitations, Archie became speedily fractious. A slipshod landlady pottered around, setting forth the crockery for dinner, while the little servant, despatched with the boy from town, mashed his dinner into an unappetizing compound on a plate. From time to time she turned to soothe him with some of the loud-voiced facetiæ peculiar to the little servant species in its dealings with fretful childhood, and at these moments Carew suspended his meditations on his quondam mistress to wish for the presence of his wife. It was only the second day of his son's visit to him, and his unfamiliarity with the arrangement was not without its effect upon his nerves.

Dissatisfied by temperament, his capacity for enjoying the past was proportionately keen, and, reflectively consuming a chop in full view of the unappetizing compound and infancy's vagaries with a spoon, he proceeded to re-live it, discerning in the process a thousand charms to which the reality had seen him blind.

Nor was he able to shake off the influence of the encounter when dinner was done. Fancifully, while the child scrambled in a corner with some toys, he installed Mary in the room; imagining his condition if he had married her, and moodily watching his clouds of smoke as they sailed across the dirty dishes. 'Damn it!' he exclaimed, rising to his feet. Such titillation of the mind was productive of the desire for a further meeting, and, but for the conviction that the endeavours would be futile, he would have gone at once into the streets.

That he would see her again before he left the place he was determined, but he failed to do so both on the morrow and the next day, albeit he extended his promenade beyond its usual limits. He did not in these excursions fail to remark that a town sufficiently large to divide one hopelessly from the face one seeks, can yet be so small that the same strangers' countenances are recurrent at nearly every turn. A coloured gentleman he anathematized especially for his iteration.

Though he doubted the possibility of the thing, he could not rid himself of the idea that she would be at the theatre some evening, impelled by the temptation to look upon him without his know-

ledge; and he played his best now on the chance
she might be there. As often as was practicable,
he scanned the house during the progress of the
piece, and between the acts inspected it through
the peep-hole in the curtain.

Noticing his observations one night, a pretty girl
in the ' wings ' asked jocularly if ' *she* had promised
to wait outside for him.'

'No, Kitty, my darling, she hasn't; she won't
have anything to do with me!' he answered, and
would have liked to stop and flirt with her. His
brain was hot in the instant, and one woman or
another just then——

If Mary had indeed been waiting, he could have
talked to her as sentimentally as before. He would
have felt as much sentiment too, such passing
attention as that diminishing his stock of it in no
degree, but rather heightening it, any compunction
for the indulgence experienced subsequently being
assuaged by a general condemnation of masculine
nature.

The pretty girl had no part in the play. She was the daughter of a good-looking woman who filled the dual capacity of chambermaid and wardrobe-mistress. Albeit she had only just left boarding-school, however, it was a foregone con-clusion that, like her mother, she would be connected with the lower branches of the pro-fession before very long. Already she had acquired very perfectly, in private, the 'burlesque-lady' tone of address, and was not unacquainted with the interiors of certain provincial bars, where her parent was addicted to taking what she termed her 'nightcap' after the performance.

Carew discovered them both, among a group of the male members of the company, in the little back-parlour of an adjacent public-house an hour later. Kitty, innocent enough as yet to find 'darling' a novelty, welcomed his advent with a flash of her eyes; but to this overture he gave no response, and, sipping his whisky, abandoned him-self to reverie until the others commented on his abstraction. He replied morosely, and, emptying his glass at a gulp, called for it to be refilled. It was not unusual for him now to drink to excess— he was accustomed to excuse the weakness by compassionating himself upon his dreary life—and to-night he lay back on the settee imbibing whisky, until his voice was heard above the rest at last, in the loquacity which preludes intoxication.

They remained at the table long after the hour for closing; the landlady, who was a friend of Kitty's mamma, enjoining them to quietude, and appearances being maintained without their removal. She was not averse to joining the party herself when the lights in the window had been extinguished, nor did Kitty decline a glass of wine either when pressed by Carew to be sociable.

'Because you're growing up,' he said with a foolish laugh—' " getting a big girl now " !'

She swept him a mock obeisance in the centre of the floor, shaking back the hair that still hung loose about her shoulders.

'Sherry,' she said, 'if mother says her "popsy" may! Because I'm "getting a big girl now," mother!'

The bar was in darkness, and this necessitated investigation with a box of matches. When the bottle was produced, it proved to be empty, the girl's pantomime of despair being received with loud guffaws. Everybody had drunk more than was advisable, and the proprietress again attempted to restrain the hilarity by feeble allusions to her licence.

'The sherry's in the cupboard down the passage!' she exclaimed; 'won't you have something else instead? Now, do make less noise, there's good boys; you'll get me into trouble!'

'I'll go and get it,' said Kitty, breaking into a momentary step-dance, with uplifted arms. 'Trust me with the key?'

'And *I'll* go and see she doesn't rob you,' cried Carew. 'Come along, Kit!'

'Not you,' said her mother; 'she'll do best

alone!' But the remonstrance was unheeded, and, as the girl ran out into the passage, he followed, till, as they reached the cupboard and stood fumbling at the lock, he caught her round the waist and kissed her.

They came back with the bottle together, in the girl's bearing an assertion of complacent womanhood evoked by the indignity. Carew applied himself to the liquor with renewed diligence, and by the time the gathering dispersed circumspectly through the private door, his eyes were glazed.

The sleeping town stretched before his uncertain footsteps blanched in moonlight as he bade the others a thick 'good-night,' and, with inebriety's lowered brows and fixity of stare, took his way towards home. It was a mile and more distant, and, muddled by the potations, he struck into the wrong road, pursuing and branching from it impetuously, until Westport wound itself around him in all the confusion of a maze. Once he paused beside a doorway, fancying he heard the tread of an approaching pedestrian who might direct him; but the sound, if sound there had been, became no clearer, and, his head grown heavier with the air, he wandered on again, ultimately with no effort to divine his situation. The sun was rising when, partially sobered, he passed through the cottage-gate at length. The sea lapped gently on the sand under a flushing sky, but in the bedroom a candle burned still, and it was in the flare of this that the little servant confronted him with a frightened face.

'Master Archie, sir!' she faltered; 'I've been up with him all night—he's ill!'

'Ill?' He stood stupidly on the threshold, looking at her. 'What do you mean by ill? what is it?'

'I don't know, sir; I don't know what I ought to do; I think he ought to have a doctor.'

He pushed past her, with a muttered ejaculation, to where the child lay whimpering and tossing on the bed.

'What's the matter, Archie? What is it, little chap?'

'It's his neck he complains of,' she murmured; 'you can see it's all swollen. He can't eat anything.'

The father passed his fingers round the tiny throat, gazing about him in dismay. Affection for a child never works a transformation in a man's character, though love for a woman may do it in exceptional cases; but the firmest devotion he could know Carew had given to his son, and now a dread of losing him, a sudden terror of his own incompetence, gripped his heart.

'Fetch someone,' he stammered; 'go, and bring a doctor back with you. Good Lord! why did I have him down?'

He sank on to the edge of the mattress, pressing his hand across his brow as if to smooth away the fumes of liquor from his understanding. A basin of water was on the washstand, and he rose and plunged his head into its depths. While he waited the stir of awakening life began to mingle with the quietness. Through the window came the clatter of feet in the neighbouring yard, the rattle of a pail upon the stone. He contemplated the languid features, conscience-stricken by his own condition, the inappropriateness of which appeared to intensify the gravity of the child's, and strove to allay his anxiety by repeated questions, to which he obtained peevish and unsatisfactory replies.

It was upwards of two hours before the girl returned. She was accompanied by a practitioner in whose attire the signs of a hasty toilette were plainly visible. Carew watched his examination eagerly, vaguely relieved by the professional calm.

‘ Is it serious ?’ he demanded.

‘ It looks like diphtheria, but it's early yet to say. He has a splendid constitution ; that's half the battle. Mother a good physique? So I should have thought! Are you a resident in the town, sir ?’

'I'm an actor; I'm in an engagement here; my wife's abroad. Why do you ask?'

The doctor included the artist and the room in an abstracted glance.

'The little one had better be removed,' he said, buttoning his coat; 'there's danger of infection with diphtheria: lodgings won't do. Take him to the hospital, and have him properly looked after. It'll be best for him in every way.'

'I am much obliged for your advice,' Carew answered hesitatingly. 'I shall be here myself for another week at least,' he added, in allusion to the fee. 'Is it safe to move him, do you think?'

'Oh yes, no need to fear that. Wrap him up, and take him away in a fly this morning. The sooner the better. . . . Not at all, my dear sir. Good-day to you.'

He departed blithely with an appetite for breakfast, and Carew went slowly back to the bed where Archie remained crying at the stranger's touch.

'Archie will have a nice drive,' he said, modu-

lating his voice to a tone of dreary encouragement
—' a nice drive in a carriage with papa.'

' I'se tired,' said the child, ' I'se sleepy.'

' A nice drive out in the sunshine, and see the
sea.' He moistened his lips with his drink-furred
tongue. ' Nurse will put on your clothes.'

' I'se seen the sea, I don't want !'

And Carew's own distaste to the proposed
arrangement was increased by the sight of the
efforts to resist. It was not in the first few
minutes that this abrupt presentment of the
hospital to the man's mind recalled Mary's connection with it, and when the recollection flashed back
to him his spirits lightened. If the boy was really
to be laid up, away from his mother's relatives in
London, he felt it could hardly be under happier
circumstances than to be ill where—— The reflection faded to a question-point. *Would* she be of
use ? Could he expect or dare to ask for tenderness
from Mary Brettan—and to the other woman's
child ? He doubted it.

In the revulsion of feeling that followed that
leaping hope, he almost determined to withhold
the request.   Many people's children were safe in
a hospital; why not his?   He would pay for
everything.   And then he sickened at the thought
of the frailty of the life he was told to leave to the
tendance of strange hands—the little form that
seemed to him, in its sickness, to have become
smaller still, and more fragile.

The difference between the careless and the fond
is often but a difference of duration, and in Carew's
impulsive emotion of the present there was the
same sincerity that would have been experienced
by the best of men.   As he lay back in the jolting
vehicle with Archie in his arms, he debated again
and again a plea to Mary to be kind to him,
daunted by the outrage of such an appeal, and
wrestling with the shame of it for the sake of the
benefit it would give his boy.   Without knowing
what she could do, he was sensible that her interest
would be valuable.   He clung passionately to the

idea of quitting the hospital with the knowledge
that it contained a friend, an individual who would
spare to the little fellow something more than the
patient's equitable and purchased due.

The cab halted with a jerk, and still revolving
the point he went into the empty waiting-room.
It was a gaunt, narrow apartment on the ground-
floor, with an expanse of glass, like the window of
a shop, overlooking the street. He sat Archie in a
corner of one of the forms ranged against the walls,
and, pending the appearance of the house-surgeon,
played nervously with the cover of an old volume
of an illustrated paper on the table. The minutes
of delay lagged drearily. He recollected on a
sudden that it could happen the symptoms might
be pronounced quite trifling, a consideration that
occurred to him for the first time, but which
vanished, almost as it came, under the influence of
the surroundings. The bare melancholy of the
walls chilled him anew, and the suggestion of
poverty about the place added to his misgivings.

He thought he would resolve to speak to her ; if she refused he would have done no harm. And she would not refuse, she was so good. Yes, she had always been a good woman. He remembered——

The handle of the door turned abruptly, and he rose in the presence of Kincaid. The eyes of the two men met for an instant in a questioning glance.

' Your child ?' said Kincaid, advancing.

Carew made assent.

' It is his neck,' he explained. ' I was advised to bring him here, because I am only in lodgings in the town. I should wish him——'

' Let me see !' An interval of suspense ensued. Carew resumed his seat, his gaze dwelling upon the doctor's movements, every detail of professional procedure twanging on his nerves. A nurse was called in to take the temperature. He watched her breathlessly, and smiled feebly at the babe across her arm. ' Diphtheritic throat ! We'll put him to bed at once. Take him into a special ward, nurse.'

'I should like——' said Carew huskily. 'One of the nurses here is known to me—might I be allowed to see her?'

'Yes, certainly; which one?'

'Her name is Brettan—Mary Brettan.' He stooped to caress the tearful face as it was carried forth, and the other's indication of surprise escaped him. 'If she is disengaged——'

Kincaid spoke to the retiring woman.

'See if Nurse Brettan can come down, please,' he said. 'Say she is wanted in the waiting-room.'

A brief pause followed the withdrawal. The closing of the door left them alone, and both remained standing silently. The father's imagination pursued the figures that had disappeared; Kincaid's was busy with the fact of the man being an acquaintance of Mary's—the only acquaintance who had crossed his path. Surprise suggested his opening remark.

'You are a visitor in the town, you say?' he observed. 'Your little son's sickness has come at an unfortunate time for you.'

'It has—yes, very. I am playing at the theatre, and my apartments are none too good.'

He mentioned the address, and the doctor made some formal inquiries. Carew asked how often he could be permitted to see the boy, and when this was arranged, silence fell again.

It was interrupted in a few seconds. The sound of a footstep on the stairs was caught by them simultaneously. Simultaneously both men looked round in the direction whence it came. The footstep was succeeded by the faint rustle of a skirt, and Nurse Brettan moved across the threshold of the room. She started visibly, controlling herself, and acknowledging Carew's greeting by a slight bow.

Kincaid in a manner presented him to her—courteously, constrainedly.

'This gentleman has been waiting to see you,' said he. 'I will wish you good-morning, sir.'

The woman went over to the window, and stood there without speaking. In the print and linen costume of the house she recalled to Carew with increased force the days of their earliest meeting.

'Archie has got diphtheria,' he said; 'he's just been taken upstairs.'

'I am sorry!' she rejoined. 'Why have you asked for me?'

'They said I could not keep him at home—that he must be brought to the hospital. Mary, you will do what you can for him?'

She raised her head calmly.

'He is sure of careful nursing,' she answered; 'none of the patients are neglected.'

'I know—I know all that. I thought you——'

'I am not in the children's ward,' she said; 'there is nothing in my power.'

He confronted her dumbly. Indifference by itself his agitation would have found vent in com-

bating, but the conclusiveness of the reply left
him nothing to urge.

'I must be satisfied without you, then,' he said
at last. 'I thought of you directly.'

'He will have every attention; you need not
doubt that.'

'Such a little chap—among strangers!'

'We have very young children in the wards.'

'And perhaps to be dangerously ill!'

'You should try to hope for the best.'

'Ah, you speak like the hospital nurse to me!'
he cried; 'I remembered the woman!'

'I speak to you like what I am!' she returned
coldly; 'I *am* one of the nurses. Myself, I have
no remembrances.'

'You could remember this week when we met
again. And once you would not have found it so
impossible to spare a minute's kindness to my
boy!'

She moved towards the door, paler, but self-
contained.

'1 must leave you now,' she said; 'I am not able to remain away very long.'

'You choose to forget only when something is asked of you.'

'I have told you,' she said, turning, 'that it is out of my power to do anything.'

'And you are glad you can truthfully say it.'

'Perhaps. No reminder of my old disgrace is pleasant to me.'

'Your reformation is a very complete one,' he answered bitterly; 'the woman I used to know would have been unable to retaliate upon a helpless child.'

The sting of the retort roused her to refutation. Her hand, which had been extended towards the handle, dropped to her side; she faced him swiftly.

'You find me what you made of me!' she said with white lips. 'I neither retaliate nor pity; what is your wife's child to me, that you ask my care of it? If I am hard, it was you who taught me hardness before ever he was born!'

'It is *my* child I asked your care for; and I brought myself to ask it because he's my dearest thing on earth. I thank God to learn he won't be in your charge!'

She shivered—he saw the shiver in her features —and for a moment looked at him intently. Then her eyelids drooped, and she left him without a word.

She went out into the corridor—her hand was pressed against her breast—but the routine the interview had broken was not immediately resumed. She made her way into the children's wing, moving with nothing of indecision in her manner, but like one who proceeds to fulfil a settled purpose. The beds, side by side in two rows, left a passage down the middle of the floor, and through this she walked, scanning the avenue of faces, until she reached the nurses' table.

As it chanced, it was to the one Kincaid had summoned that she addressed herself:

'There's a boy just been brought in with

diphtheria, Sophie; do you know where he is ?'

' Yes, I'm going back to him in a minute. He's in a special ward.'

' Let me see him !'

' Have you got permission ?'

' No.'

Nurse Gay hesitated.

' I shall get into trouble,' she said. ' Why don't you ask for it ?'

' I don't want to wait; I want to see him now !'

' I've been in hot water once this week already——'

' Sophie, I know the mite, and—and his people. I *must* go in to him !'

The girl glanced at her sharply, startled by something in her voice.

' Oh, if it comes to that,' she said, ' it's only a " wigging "—go !' And she told her whereabouts he was.

He lay, when Mary entered, alone in the simple

room—a diminutive patient for whom the narrow cot seemed large. The nurse had been showing him a picture-book; and this yawned loosely on the quilt, where it had slid, during her absence, from the languid hold. At the sound of Mary's approach he turned, as if in hope the other had returned, but, meeting with a countenance he did not recognise, sighed weakly, a doubtful gaze appraising her intentions.

At first she did not speak. She stooped over the pillow, smoothing and re-smoothing it mechanically, a hand trembling closer to the warmth of the disordered curls. Her own gaze deepened and hung upon him; her lips parted. Her hands crept timidly nearer, and rested on the little head entirely, till the quiver of its pulses stirred under her touch. Gradually her bosom drooped, until her mouth was yielding kisses on his cheek. She yearned over him through wet lashes, with the wondering smile always on her face.

'Archie,' she murmured; 'Archie, baby-boy, is

it "comfy" for you? Won't you see the pictures —all the pretty people in the book?'

'Show more pictures,' he said wearily, 'others, to me!'

'You shall have others this afternoon, dear,' she answered; 'this afternoon, when I go out. Let me show you these now! See, there's a little boy in bed, like you. Such a nice little boy; his name was "Archie," too, and one day papa took him to a big house, where papa had friends, and——'

'Papa! I *want* papa!'

'Oh, my darling,' she said, 'papa is coming! He will come very, very soon. The other little boy wanted papa just as you do, and he wasn't happy at first at all. But in the big house—the same as this—everybody was so kind, and glad to have Archie, that presently he was quite pleased to stop. It was so nice directly; it was better than at home. They gave him toys, and lots and lots of picture-books; and on the table there were oranges and puddings—it was beautiful!'

She reviewed, meanwhile, the father's plead-ing eyes, red with the marks of whisky, which she commiserated as the evidence of a watchful night.

It was impossible to remain, she was needed elsewhere; and when Kincaid made the matutinal round she was on duty. But she ascertained the developments throughout the day almost as they came, and she knew by twilight that the child was grievously unwell. She did not marvel at her interest. It engrossed her to the exclusion of astonishment. If she was surprised at all, it was that Carew could have believed in her neutrality, the assumption of which sustained her miserably in recollection, even while she joyed to reflect that his first impulse had been to put faith in her good heart. She did not, as she might have done, submit the passion of sympathy to analysis, ashamed of the cause from which it sprang. When she had gazed during the intervening years at the faded photograph kept since the farewell, she had reproached herself and wept. Now it all seemed natural. She sought neither to reason nor to euphemize. The feeling was spontaneous, and she went with it. She called it by no wrong word, because she called it nothing. She was borne as it carried her, blindly and unresistingly, without pausing to name it or to define its source. It seemed quite natural. She inquired about Archie when she had risen next morning, contriving a little later another flying visit to the room ; but he was now too ill to notice her, and she quitted him unrelieved by the inspection.

Carew came again that afternoon ; she learnt it while he still was there, and gathered—affecting indifferent concern—something of his wretchedness. She heard how he besieged the nurse with questions : 'whether she had seen so bad a case before—well, often before ? Were those who recovered so young as this one ? Was there nothing else that could be tried?' She listened, her head bowed, imagining the scene she could not

enter ; deploring, remembering, re-living—praying
for ' Tony's son.'

Not, however, until after the man had gone was
everything that had occurred related to her. She
was sitting at the extremity of the ward, sewing,
shortly to be free for the night. It was the hour
when the quietude of hospital atmosphere begins to
deepen into the perceptible hush which preludes
the extinction of the patients' lights. The tea-
trays had long since been removed from the
bedsides. Through the apertures of curtain a few
of the occupants, loath to waive the privilege while
they held it, were to be seen immersed in books
and magazines ; but others had succumbed to
sleep already, and even the most convalescent, the
late-birds of the ward who dissipated in wheel-
chairs to the admiration of the rest, had suspended
their excursions till the morrow. The Major—
nicknamed the ' Watchman '—who executed his
peregrinations in a dressing-gown, had stopped
before the last opening, and wished the last of the

wakeful ones 'a comfortable night, sir.' The chess champion had concluded his final conquest on a recumbent adversary's quilt. Where breakfast comes at six o'clock, grown men resume some of the habits of their infancy, and the day that begins so early closes soon. It was very peaceful, very still, and she was sitting in the lamp-rays, sewing.

She looked round as the matron joined her. Her interest in the case was known, and the two commenced to talk in subdued voices.

'How is he?'

'He's been dreadfully bad! The worst of it took place before the father left: Dr. Kincaid had to come up.'

'What?—tell me!'

'He had to perform tracheotomy. The father was there all the time; Dr. Kincaid explained to him what was going to be done, and he wouldn't go. The child was blue in the face, and there wasn't any stopping to argue! When the cut was made in the throat, and the tube put in, I never

saw a man turn colour so! I was standing just by
him, and he caught hold of my arm. "My God,"
he said, "will he breathe easier through that?
Won't it hurt him?" I told him it was the only
way of enabling the mite to fetch his breath at all,
but he scarcely seemed to hear me. The tears
were running down his face, and when the boy
burst into a fit of coughing—you know the sort of
coughing that follows——'

'Yes, yes, what then?'

'He thought he was going to die. He broke
down altogether, and the doctor ordered him out of
the room. "If you're fond of your son, keep quiet
here, sir," he said, "or go and compose yourself
outside!" I think he was sorry he'd spoken so
sternly afterwards, though he was quite right,
for——'

'Oh,' murmured Mary, 'this is ghastly!'

The canvas opposite had been adorned with the
presentation 'plate' of a 'Summer Number,' and
she sat staring at it fixedly, cold and damp.

'I went out after him,' pursued the other, 'and comforted him as much as I could. He took both my hands and patted them like a girl. "You're a good woman," he said—"a good woman. I'd no business to have stopped; I haven't the nerves for it! But I'm glad I was there: whatever happens, I shall always think it was right I was there, don't you?" I said he must try to believe that only the best was going to happen now; though whether I was right to say it, God knows! When it comes to tracheotomy in diphtheria, the child's chance—— Still, this one is as fine a little fellow as ever I saw; he's the strength of many a pair we get here. And the man was in such a state of mind I could have cried for him! When he had to leave—he had to hurry off to the theatre to act—he was just as white as a sheet. How he'll get through I can't imagine! He's coming back to-night directly he finishes; he's to see *me*, if he doesn't see the child.'

'I must go!' exclaimed Mary; 'I must go to the

ward!' She rose, pressing her hands together convulsively. 'I can go in to him, can't I? It is Nurse Mainwaring's time to relieve me—why isn't she here?'

The matron calmed her considerately.

'Hush! you can go to him as soon as she comes,' she said; 'don't " take on," or I shall be sorry I told you. Nurse Bradley has complained of feeling ill; I expect she is delayed by that.'

Mary raised a faint smile, deprecating her vehemence.

'I am very fond of the boy,' she answered, with apology in her tones; 'I thank you for thinking of telling me very much.'

The looked-for woman now appeared.

'Nurse Bradley is unable to get up, madam,' she announced.

'Nonsense! what is it?'

'A sick-headache; she can't see out of her eyes.'

There was the consternation that always falls in a hospital when one of the staff is indisposed—the interregnum of dismay, during which the rest gaze blankly in their neighbours' faces.

'Then we are short-handed to-night. You relieve here, Nurse Mainwaring?'

'Yes, madam.'

'And Nurse Gay—who should relieve her?'

'Nurse Bradley.'

'*I* will relieve her,' declared Mary; 'I ask for nothing better.'

'You need your night's rest as much as most. And there's no napping with "trachy"—it means a continual watch.'

'I shall not nap; I shall not wish to. Somebody must lose her night's rest—why not I?'

'I think we can manage without you.'

'It will be a favour to me. I am grateful for the opportunity.'

'Well, then, you shall halve it with someone. You can take the first half, and——'

'No,' she urged, 'that is hard on the other, and no grace to me. Give it me all.'

The matron solved the dilemma :

' Nurse Brettan relieves Nurse Gay.'

In the room the boy lay motionless, as if already
dead. From the mouth breath no longer passed,
and only by a hand placed before the opening of
the tube inserted in the childish throat could it be
detected by sensation that he now breathed at all.
As Mary took her place by his side the force of
professional training displayed itself in the most
practical form. She had begged for the extra duty
with almost feverish excitement; she entered upon
it collected and self-controlled. A stranger would
have said : ' A conscientious woman, but experience
has blunted her sensibilities.'

On the table were some feathers, with one of
which she would from time to time throughout
the night be required to keep the tube free from
obstruction. Indulgence, however brief, to an
attack of drowsiness was under the circumstances
impossible. To devote unwavering attention to
the state of the passage through which air was

admitted to the lungs was not merely important, the necessity was vital. A rigid, a never-ceasing vigilance was required. It was to this the nurse, already worn by the usual duties of the day, had pledged herself in default of the absentee.

At half-past nine she had cleansed the tube twice. At ten Kincaid appeared. She rose as he came in.

'I am relieving Nurse Gay,' she said; 'Nurse Bradley is indisposed.'

He went to the cot and ascertained that all was well.

'It will be very trying for you; was there no one to divide the work?'

'I wanted to do it all myself.'

'Ah yes, I understand; you know the father.'

It was the first reference to the other's request for her that he had made, and she was sensible of some inquiry in his tone. She bowed mutely; and, in the only occasion during which he had been alone with her since her appointment, they stood together looking at Carew's son.

She had no wish to speak. On him who could have said much the situation imposed restraint, though to be with her thus had yet its fascination to him : a vague charm not to be uttered, not to be dwelt on, but a sentiment of confidential intercourse, due in part to the prevailing silence of the house, such as he had not felt with her before.

While they looked, the boy gave a quick gasp. The tube had become clogged.

Mary started spasmodically, throwing out her arm for the feather; but Kincaid had been before her, favoured by his position.

' All right !' he said; ' I will free it.'

He leant over the pillow, feather in hand. She watched him steadfastly, her eyes widening in terror, for she saw his endeavours were futile, and he could not free it.

The waxen placidity of the upturned face vanished as she watched. Labouring for breath, it regained the signs of life to struggle with the gripe of death —distorted in an instant, and distorted frightfully. An ordinary woman would have wept aloud. The nurse, to all intents and purposes, preserved her calmness still.

It was Kincaid who gave the first signal of despondence.

' The thing is blocked !' he exclaimed ; ' I cannot clear it !'

His voice had the repressed despair of a surgeon who is also an enthusiast confronted by a higher and opposing force. Under the test of his defeat her composure broke down. Amidst a danger in which her interest was vivid and personal she—as the father had done before her—became agitated and unstrung.

' You must !' she answered. ' Doctor, for God's sake !'

He was still striving, but with scant success.

' I am doing my utmost,' he said ; ' it seems no good !'

'You must save this life!' she repeated; 'you will?'

'I have said I can do no more.'

'You will—you shall!' she persisted wildly. The very passion of motherhood suffused her features. 'Doctor, it is *his* child!'

He looked at her; he looked at her once even then. Their eyes met in a flash across the cot; there was no room for more. The gasps of the dying baby became abruptly horrible to witness. The eyeballs rolled hideously, seeming as if they would spring from their sockets. The tiny chest heaved and fell in frequent and agonizing efforts to gain air, while in its convulsive battle against suffocation the frail body almost lifted itself from the mattress.

'Go away!' said the man huskily; 'there is nothing you can do!'

She refused to stir. She appealed to him with desperate gaze.

'Help him!' she stammered.

'There is no way!'

'Do you, the doctor, tell me there is no way?'

'I tell you, none!'

'But *I* know there *is* a way!' she cried resolutely. 'I can suck that tube!'

'Mary! My God! it might kill you!'

She flung herself forward, but the conflict ceased as he withheld her. A small quantity of the mucus had been dislodged by the paroxysm it had produced. Nature had done—imperfectly, but still done—what science had failed to effect: the child breathed again.

The outbreak was followed by complete exhaustion, and once more it seemed that life was already extinct. Kincaid assured himself it still lingered, and turned to her gravely.

'You were about to do a wicked and a foolish thing. After what it has gone through, nothing under heaven can save the child; you ought to know it. At best you could only hope to prolong his life for two or three hours.'

She was crying great tears. They fell on the heart of the man who loved her, and burnt there with the cause.

' "Only!" ' she said brokenly; ' do you think that is nothing to me? An hour longer, and the father will be here—to find him living or dead! Do you suppose I can't imagine—do you suppose I don't feel—what *he* feels there on the stage while he counts each moment for the blessing of release? In an hour the curtain will have fallen, and he will have rushed here with a prayer to be in time. If it were revealed that I should do nothing but prolong the life by the sacrifice of mine, I would sacrifice it! Gladly, proudly—yes, proudly—as God hears! You could never have prevented me; nothing should prevent me! I would risk my life ten times rather than he should arrive too late!'

' This,' murmured her lover drearily, ' is the return you would make for his sin!'

' No,' she said; ' it is the atonement I would offer for mine!'

He stood dumbly at the head of the cot; the woman trembled at the foot. But they saw the change next minute simultaneously. For the second and last time the passage had become hopelessly clogged. She gave a hoarse cry, and darted to the vacant side. He could not hinder her. He spoke.

' Stop ! Nurse Brettan, I order you to leave the ward !'

The voice rang true, and an instant she wavered; but it was the veriest instant. The woman had vanquished the nurse, and the woman was the stronger now. A glance sped at him of mingled supplication and defiance, and, casting herself on the bed, she set her lips to the tube !

CHAPTER XIV.

It was the work of a moment. Almost as he started forward to restrain her, she had raised herself, and, burying her face in a handkerchief, leant, shaking, against the wall.

Kincaid gazed at her, white and stern, and a tense silence ensued, broken by her:

'You can have me dismissed,' she said; 'he will see his child!'

He answered nothing. The cruelty of the speech that ignored and perverted everything outside the interests of the man by whom she had been wronged seemed the last blow his pain could have to bear. A sense of the injustice and inequality of life's distribution overwhelmed him. Viewed in

the light of her defeated enemy, he felt as broken,
as far from dignity or power, as if the imputation
had been just.

She resumed her seat, and, lingering so long as
duty still demanded, he at length ejected some
required remark. She replied constrainedly; the
intervention of the pause was demonstrated by their
tones, which sounded flat and dull. He was
thankful when he could retire, nor was his withdrawal less welcome to the woman, to whose
reactionary weakness the removal of supervision
came as balm. He went heavily from her, and
she drew her chair yet closer to the bedside; the
subsiding exaltation of her mood echoed from her
relief at his departure.

Carew would see his boy; she had no other
settled thought, save an averse remembrance that
he must perforce see her as well. The reflection that
he would hear of her share in the matter gladdened
her scarcely at all; indeed, when she contemplated
his enlightenment, she was bashful and perturbed.

He would learn that his original faith in her had been justified, and he would be sorry—piteously sorry—for all the hard words that he had used. But by herself there was little to be gained : what she had done had been for him. She found it even a humiliation to think that her jeopardizing her life would be known to him—a humiliation which his gratitude would do nothing to decrease. She consulted the watch she had pawned for the rent of her garret after his renunciation of her, and determined the length of time before he could arrive.

The stress of the last few minutes could not be suffered to beget any abatement of wariness. But by degrees, as the reverberation of the outburst faded, she felt more tranquil than she had done since the matron joined her earlier in the evening ; and she continued the vigil with undiminished care. Archie would die—she bewailed the edict, foreseeing the shock of the death upon another— but now the father would be present at least. The closing moments would not pass while he was simulating misery or mirth upon a stage. Horror of the averted fate, more dreadful to a woman's mind even than to the father's own, made this brief protraction appear an almost priceless boon.

It was possible for him to be here already; scarcely likely, perhaps, so soon as this, but possible, supposing that the piece 'played quick,' and a cab had been ordered to await him at the door. She listened for the roll of wheels in the distance, but the quietude was undisturbed. Archie was lying as calmly as when she had entered. Assuming no further impediments occurred to exhaust the remaining strength more speedily, it seemed safe to infer he might last two hours.

Her misgivings anent her risk were slight. The danger she had run might prove fatal; contrariwise, it need do nothing of the kind. Similar deeds had been performed with impunity—she had heard of one, at any rate, and she recalled it. In her own case a serious result looked exceedingly unlikely, because in health catastrophes to other people always appear more probable than to one's self, and she regarded the benefit acquired by her temerity as being cheaply bought. None, however, knew better than she how much completive attention was called for, what alertness of eye and hand was essential when the act was done; and, sitting there, her gaze was fastened on the boy as if she sought to hearken to every flutter of his pulse.

Now a cab did approach, and she caught her breath as it rattled near. It stopped, she fancied, before the hospital gate. Still with the stare riveted on the unconscious child, she strained her ears for the confirmatory tread. The seconds ticked away, swelling to minutes, and no footstep fell. The hope had been illusive, for presently the conveyance was heard again, in driving off. She began to grow impatient and distressed. Allowing a margin for a too sanguine calculation, it was time the man was here! Once admitting the delay to be unaccountable, no conjecture could be formed as to its extent. Her fingers were laced and unlaced nervously in her lap. She conceived the rumble of cab-wheels in the soughing of the wind, intent and discomfited alternately. The faint slamming of a cottage-door startled her to expectation. In the intensity of the hush, that sank with every subsidence of sound, she could feel the throbbing of her heart.

Out in the town a clock struck twelve, and suspense verged upon despair. Her eyes now hung upon the boy, haggard with desperation; she leant over him in an absorption of solicitude, ready to contest the advent of the end inch by inch. So far no change was shown. Carew might find him living even yet! A prayer that it should be so rose from her, unformulated and imploring. Racked with anticipation and despondence, tortured by the fear that what she had done might, after all, be labour thrown away, she strove to devise some theory of explanation and encouragement; the confinement of her position, which debarred her excitement from the vent of unrestricted action, becoming at last an almost physical pain.

The clock struck again—one! It swept suddenly across her that the matron had seemed doubtful of letting Carew proceed to the ward on his return, and that he might have come and gone. She had been reaching forward, and her arm remained extended aimlessly. A coldness like a wave of ice-water spread through her body, and the pliability of the face left it, so that it stiffened and was undesirable to see. If during ten seconds she thought of anything but her neglect to ensure his admission, she thought she felt the blood dripping away in little pin-pricks from her cheeks. The solution banished the shred of hope to which she had yet clung, and, thwarted by her own oversight, frustration · paralyzed the woman. Her enterprise now assumed an aspect of grievous hazard, enhanced by its futility. She lifted herself faint at soul. Her ministrations were instinctive, mechanical. She resumed the offices, she was assiduous and watchful, but she appeared to herself prompted by the volition of another, operated by some outside influence, with her mind half numbed.

In the midst of this a new hope thrilled her abruptly. She heard the stroke of three, and the boy was living still. The leaping thought she was afraid to welcome shook her back to ardour. She tried to put it aside; she said it was vain, chimerical. She tried to believe it had been a transient fancy without power to support her. But it had sent the colour rushing to her neck and brow, and her hands were hot. She sat strained with the intensity of what she trembled to acknowledge. Each minute that might bring the end, and yet withheld it, saw her regard more fixed. Each minute meant encouragement that gripped her with its force. Time crept, debilitated by the fever of suspense. Between eternities the distant clock rang forth the quarters, hollow and reverberant, across the sleeping town, and at every quarter she gasped ' Thank God !' and wondered would she thank Him by the next. She dreaded each quiver of her lashes that veiled the boy from view, as if the spark of life would vanish as her eyelids fell. When her gaze wavered her own strength failed her, but she was sustained, and felt sustaining, with it bent. At her waist the watch she would not look at ticked, and ticked in wild exaggeration of time's flight. The laggard clock boomed confutation sullenly, dispelling the idea it must have stopped. Hour merged into hour, and he lingered on. Cramped, but unswerving, she could have shrieked her prayer aloud. The dreariness of coming day lightened the blind before the bed; the light grew clearer, and he lingered still. There was the stir of morning; people moved along the street. Dawn touched him with its grayness while he tarried yet. And when at last the sun uprose it found him breathing peacefully once more. And then she knew that Heaven had worked a miracle, and the child would live.

Among the Westport staff that case is cited now, and to-day they tell the tale how Mary Brettan saved a life. The local *Examiner* accorded the matter a third of a column, under the headline of 'Heroism by a Hospital Nurse.' And, condensed in form, the London press reported it, so that Mr. Collins, of Pattenden's, perused the paragraph—having despatched the youth of the prodigious yawn with a halfpenny—and, remembering why the surname was familiar, wondered a moment what the woman was doing who could never sell their books.

It was later in the morning when Carew entered the building, as Kincaid was crossing the hall. The brightness of the first beams had waxed into a glare. and the nervous pallor of the father's face was streaked with heat. The porter, who remarked it, heard the doctor's answer to his stammered question :

'Your son is out of danger. I am sorry to say

Nurse Mary Brettan imperilled her life to benefit him.'

Then the two men passed beyond earshot, and what followed the porter did not catch.

To Mary herself Kincaid had spoken little. He was confronted by a recovery impossible to have been conceived, but his predominant emotion was a haunting terror of its cost. She heard of Carew's gratitude from the matron, and received his message of entreaty to be allowed to see her. It was, however, not delivered until after his departure, when she awoke; and by the morrow her instinctive reluctance to an interview had deepened. She chose to content herself with the note he sent: one written to say he *could* not write, that on paper he was unable to shape his words. She read it very slowly, and it dropped to her lap, and she sat contemplating the opposite wall. Presently she smoothed her palms across her eyes, and read the lines again—more slowly, and with her eyes bent closer to the page.

Next day she rose with a strange stiffness in her throat, that increased with her descent into the ward. And she was frightened. But at first she would not mention it, because she was loath for Kincaid to know. She felt an awkwardness in drawing breath, and by noon it was not to be concealed. She went to bed protesting, but by Kincaid's command.

Nurse Brettan had become a patient. She said how queer it was to be put into the familiar room in that unfamiliar way. The girl whose watch of Archie she had relieved was deputed to attend on her; and when she was installed the invalid had rallied her weakly on the duty.

'It ought to be a good patient this spell, Sophie. If I'm fractious, you may shake me.'

But to Kincaid she spoke more earnestly now the danger-signal was displayed.

'You did all you could to stop me, doctor; whatever happens, you'll remember that. You did everything that was right, and so did I.'

'Don't talk rubbish about "happenings," nurse!' he had replied; 'we shall have you up and at work again directly.'

Nevertheless, she had grown worse as the child grew stronger; and for a fortnight the man who loved her suffered fiercer pain each time he told her 'rubbish!' And the man she loved sought daily tidings of her when he came to watch the progress of his son. She used to learn of these inquiries, and turn her face round on the pillow when they were repeated to her, and afterwards lie for a long while very quiet. Her distaste to meeting him had quite gone, and she was sick with a longing to have him come. But now she could not bring herself to do it, because her face and neck were so swollen and unsightly, and her voice had dwindled to a whisper that was not nice to hear. Then at last the hope that she would get better faded altogether, and it was known that she was dying. And one morning the nurse said to her:

'Perhaps to-day you would like to see him? He has asked again.'

'To-day?' Momentarily her eyes brightened at the notion, but the shame of her unloveliness came back to her, and she sighed. 'Give me—the glass, Sophie—there's a dear!' She looked up at her reflection in the narrow mirror held aslant over the bed. 'No,' she added feebly, 'not to-day—perhaps to-morrow!'

The girl put the glass back slowly in its place, without speaking. And the other's gaze followed her questioningly until she left.

When Kincaid came in, Mary asked him how long she had to live. He was haggard with a night of agony—a night whose marks all the nurses had observed and wondered at.

'How long?' she queried. 'I am dying, doctor, I know.' His nostrils quivered, and he clenched his teeth. 'Not—it isn't *now?*'

'Oh, don't!' he said. 'No, no! You shouldn't—you *mustn't*—frighten yourself like this!'

She was staring at him wildly, without moving.

'I am going to die!' she said; 'yes, I under-stand! To-day?'

'Not to-day,' he answered hoarsely, 'I honestly believe.'

'To-morrow?'

'Mary——'

'To-morrow?' she pleaded in the same painful whisper. 'But—to-morrow? Tell the truth!'

'I think—to-morrow you may know how much I loved you.'

She kept quite still, and he had turned aside. He noticed it was raining, and how the drops spattered on the window-sill.

'I did not see,' she murmured; 'I didn't see; I thought—you—had—forgotten.'

'No,' he said; 'you never saw. It doesn't matter; I know now it couldn't have been. Hush, dear; don't talk; it's so bad for you!'

'And I am sorry. But I was *his* before you came. I couldn't—could I?'

'No, of course,' he said. 'Don't worry; don't, for God's sake! There is nothing to be sorry about. I must go to the next ward; I shall see you in the afternoon. Try to sleep a little, won't you?'

He went out, with a word to the woman who re-entered, and Mary lay silent for many minutes. Presently she said:

'Sophie—yes, to-day!'

The nurse glanced over at her quickly.

'All right! he shall hear as soon as he comes.'

'Don't forget.'

'I won't forget; you can feel quite certain!'

'Thank you, Sophie! I am so tired!'

The rain was still falling. She could hear it blowing against the panes behind her head, and lay listening to it, wondering if it would keep him away. Then her thoughts wandered, and when Kincaid returned she was sleeping. He drew forward the vacant chair, and sat watching her until she stirred. Her eyes opened at him vaguely.

' I've been asleep ?'

' Yes.'

' Is it late ?'

' It's about three,' he said, ' I think — just three.'

' Ah !'

She closed her eyes again, and there was a long pause. He put a hand out, and covered her nerveless fingers with his own.

' Don't mind,' she whispered ; ' it doesn't hurt.'

' Oh, my dear, my dear ! My mother, and You— and powerless with both !'

' The many,' she said faintly, ' think of the many you have helped ! You have been—very good to me—very good !'

It was the third time since they met that she had told him so. And even as she spoke her ear, keener than his, had caught the footfall in the passage for which she had been waiting. And she nestled lower on the pillow, trying to hide her disfigurement from view.

'Mary,' said Kincaid, 'you didn't care for me; but will you let me kiss you on the forehead, once, while you know?'

A smile—a smile of tenderness wonderfully new and strange to him—irradiated her face for answer, and, turning, he saw the other man had come in.

THE END.

BILLING AND SONS, PRINTERS, GUILDFORD.

STORIES BY LEONARD MERRICK.

VIOLET MOSES.

'How it has fared with the Jew in modern fiction is a theme that should some day be treated by some philosophic writer as it deserves to be treated. When the hour arrives that writer cannot possibly afford to neglect Mr. Leonard Merrick's "Violet Moses." There is not the least suggestion of racial sentiment or of imperfect sympathies in Mr. Merrick's clever sketches of Jewish society in the cool sequestered Maida Vale of life. The Jew that George Eliot drew is more gratifying to the romantic eye than Mr. Leopold Moses, but the latter is unquestionably the more persuasive portraiture. Mr. Moses possesses everything—even to flesh and blood —that Mr. Deronda lacked. He is very real, in fact. In "Violet Moses" the characters are skilfully drawn, and show excellent observation, while the story altogether is notable for freshness and power.'—*Saturday Review*.

'The tendency to study real life, and the effort to portray it simply and honestly, are noticeable and satisfactory features in the fiction of to-day. "Violet Moses" is a good novel, and one that is written with taste. The scenes of the domestic life of the Hebrew community, in the class of life which the author selects for his story, are drawn with skill.'—*Observer*.

'The difficulty in novel-writing is to hit on anything original, but Mr. Merrick, so far as our pretty extensive experience goes, is fairly entitled to the honours of a discoverer. He has struck down into a new social stratum, and he seems to be at home in it. Mr. Merrick unquestionably excels as a painter of *genre*. The story is powerful and pathetic.'—*Times*.

'With a title so lucky (though luck's all my eye),
Your book's sure of readers, I'll wager my head ;
For not even a critic will dare to reply,
When he's asked to review it, "I'll take it as re(a)d."'
Punch.

'. . . The cleverness of the workmanship here and elsewhere in "Violet Moses" is unmistakable ; indeed, the book is in various ways one of the ablest of recent novels ; and if Mr. Merrick will only eschew the exclusive study of ugliness, we are sure that he has it in him to write a really fine story.'—*Spectator*.

'There is a dry matter-of-fact truthfulness about the writer's remarks which makes his story now and then delightful reading. On the whole, this is a clever and polished novel.'—*Academy*.

'Whether Maida Vale society will be gratified or not by extremely vivid portraiture may be open to doubt, but certainly the circles to which Mr. Leopold Moses introduces a very sensitive and intelligent young wife will have the charm of novelty to most of those who share the introduction.'—*Athenæum*.

'"Violet Moses" is undoubtedly a remarkable book. There are abundant touches of epigrammatic humour. At the close the situation rises to a very high pitch of tragedy.'—*Guardian*.

'Mr. Merrick's story is not only life-like and very clever, but also extremely interesting.'—*Truth*.

MR. BAZALGETTE'S AGENT.

'Mr. Leonard Merrick's book is essentially original. There is a gay freshness about its style which commends itself at once to the reader. Altogether, "Mr. Bazalgette's Agent" is a very agreeable and readable little book.'—*Era*.

'"Mr. Bazalgette's Agent" calls itself a "detective story," and is a brightly-written and very readable example of its class. The idea is eccentric, the situations are skilfully managed, and the action never halts. The story possesses the merit of a simple yet at the same time an exciting plot, and the *dénouement* is as powerful as it is startling and unexpected.'—*Wit and Wisdom*.

'The clever writer of this interesting novel may be congratulated upon having constructed a story at once full of interest and ability. The characters are full of life and reality, while the dialogue is always interesting and sometimes brilliant.'—*Society Herald*.

THE LIFE THEY SAID SHE RUINED.

Mr. Hall Caine wrote: 'Let me congratulate you upon the little story entitled "The Life they said she Ruined." It is quite admirable.'

A correspondent of *Wit and Wisdom* wrote: 'Simply as one of your readers, I must thank you for providing in your current issue such delightful reading as Leonard Merrick's "The Life they said she Ruined." Similar to the motive of this beautiful tale is that of George MacDonald's "Paul Faber," in which the ethics of the sexual relations in some aspects are finely treated. It is a pleasure to me to come across such a beautiful presentment in concrete form of my pet belief as Leonard Merrick's tale. This letter is meant as a frank expression of my thanks, and I know it will be appreciated as such.'